Paradise Is the Name of a Nearby Planet

By: Aida Musapour

Translated by: Peter Suloon

Title: Paradise Is the Name of a Nearby Planet

Author: Aida Musapour

Translator: Peter Suloon

Editor: Majid Jafari Aghdam

Publisher: Supreme Century/USA

Year of Publishing : 2020/May

No. of Pages: 194

ISBN: 9781939123985

Paradise Is the Name of a Nearby Planet

He opened his green eyes and stared at the ceiling. He had a look around. A bare girl with black hair had slept with him. He came down from the bed and removed the female's lingerie and a handbag underneath his feet. He wore his pants and stood in front of the mirror. He was tall and attractive. He took off his white shirt from the sofa and wore it. His well-built body indicated that he was an athlete. He tidied up his curly brown hair. He looked at his face in the mirror calmly and relaxed. His face was bony and handsome.

He heard the woman's sleepy voice, "When will I see you again, Brian?"

Without looking at her, he replied to her as he fastened his cufflink, "Maria...baby, you should know that last night I was with you for your urging, otherwise, you know yourself...".

Maria interrupted his saying, "It's okay, Brian. You could run away as much as you can, but I will take you."

He grinned and picked up his coat, and without saying anything, left the apartment. He pulled out his cellphone, "Send a car to the address I tell you. Don't take more than a few minutes."

Brian Werner, a thirty-year-old and attractive young, was the only son of a wealthy family and heir to one of the largest communications companies in the United States, was also one of the country's greatest financiers. He had experienced much excitement in his life. But working with NASA was the whole of his love in life that he had managed to achieve it after much study and attempt... Brian was an astronaut who had traveled to space twice to do some research until that day. He was always looking for the unattainable stuff. All of these features, along with his charming appearance and unrivaled wealth, had made him the center of attention of many beautiful, famous, and wealthy girls. And each one of them was trying to charm him, which of course he was happy with this status. He was spending almost half a day having fun with pretty girls. But he never found himself and his feelings bound to anyone.

A black BMW car stood by Brian's leg. The driver quickly got out of the car to open the door for Brian.

Brian, it is not needed. Go back to the company. I will drive myself.

- Yes, sir.

He got in the car. He was continually on the phone, working to solve various business problems. It was an old mansion. He parked the car and stood by the front door and rang the door. Then, after a few minutes, a blacky old-man opened the door for him, as he was gasping. Brian entered the home relaxed and without permission.

Old-man, Brian, what are you doing here in the morning?

- Well, I came to talk to you about my trip. Why did you open the door? No one at home?

- No. Indeed, my wife and kids have gone to Europe for the holidays. Also, I have sent my crew on leave.

Suddenly, a woman, white-skinned tall with blonde hair, came down the stairs in a vile dress.

Brian smiled mischievously and said, "Well, I think I came too untimely, dear Tom was doing the mischief..."

The man who had been becoming panic started to explain it, but when the woman approached them, he got silent again. He took some money out of his pocket and gave it to the woman. The woman put a hand on Brian's face, and without saying anything, left the house.

- What always occupies my mind is, why does someone get married, when he/she cannot commit?

"You don't know anything, boy. Marriage makes a goal for you, plus the diversity of happiness. It is not possible to put away one of them for the other." said Tom, as if the distress had gone away of him by leaving the woman.

Brian, as if had not convinced, leaned over on the couch and continued, "Leave it out... I wanted to talk to you about my trip. Honestly, I'm quite excited."

- Come on, guy. You have done it before. You shouldn't be scared.
- It is not a fear. It is a weird feeling. It's hard for me to describe it. How can I say? I feel like something is going to happen. I wish this week would be ended somehow earlier but, on the other hand.
- Brian, it's not going to have a problem. Now, come on, leave me alone. And let me have enough enjoyment of the remaining ten days of my vacation.

Brian, whose mind was heavily involved in his journey, made a faint smile.

Throughout the coming week, Brian went to see friends and had fun, until the promised morning was coming.

The voice on the phone, Hello Brian! Are you sleeping yet? We have to be in the organization half an hour later.

Brian, Okay, man. Don't worry. The launch is at 3 pm. That much excitement is not well for you at all. I will pick you up for an hour and a half later.

- Does it sound you didn't get what I said?
- You didn't hear what I said, Tom.
- Okay, so I'm waiting for you.

He got dressed and picked up a small sack. He left his room and looked down from the fences. Inside the hall, there was a lot of work, and everybody was bustling around. The servants were working in a hurry as if they were preparing something. Brian raised an eyebrow, threw his bag over his shoulder, and went down the stairs. There was a calmness in his face.

_ Hi Mom, what's going on here?

- Hi baby, could you sleep well?

- Yeah, but I still didn't understand what's going on here.

- Baby, you are not with us for ten days. You can't eat at home. I told Lara to prepare all the dishes you like.

Brian smiled. He bent down and kissed his mother's face and expressed, "Elizabeth Werner, you are the kindest and best mother in the world... but my dear, I can't eat these foods. My body must be ready."

Elizabeth wiped her tears and reacted, "Oh, my son, when do you want to give up these deeds, you are the heir to Werner's family. Our family needs you. Every time you set off for a mission, and we cannot find you, I'm going to die and revive. You are surfing the earth and space. You are at home only one month among the twelve months of the year. You have to get married after this trip."

- No, Mom.

- That's that. When you return, you have to get married. I am going to choose some candidates from prominent government families during this time.

Brian laughed, "Mommy, are we trading? I have to marry a girl whom I love her. Love gives meaning to life, otherwise, that every animal knows reproduction and does it."

- You won't be fall in love with anyone till the end of your life. You are just looking for pleasure and fun, and that's it.

- Okay, Mom. So, choose for me one of the most beautiful.

He laughed and went to the table; he picked up an apple and started to walk across the home. He called his agent, Albert, and explained everything to him.

- Albert, talk to lawyers and justify them about what I asked you to do. In my absence, things must do well.

- Don't worry. Be sure, sir.

- I'm sure, Albert. All the documents have signed, and my shares have transferred to my mother through my will. I don't want her to have any problems after my death, and you are not allowed to have an interview in the mass media.

- Okay, sir. By the way, Miss Marie has sent a bunch of flowers for you and has mentioned that she will come to see you off.

- No, Albert. How can I get rid of this girl?

Albert got silent.

- All right, Albert. I'll find a solution for her.

The house was an aristocratic mansion and decorated with antique items. Brian explored the entire house and looked everywhere, entered the workroom, and drew his hand on his father's Russian desk.

He had a look at the books and then went to the living room. Sad Elizabeth was sitting on a sofa, and one of the crew was massaging her palm.

- What's up, Brian? It seems you are somehow weird today.

- What do you mean? Every time I go on a lengthy mission, I look at the house thoroughly because I will miss it. Whenever I take a risky trip, I do a few things for a caution aspect. Anyway, we have to remember that I'm not an ordinary fellow, Mommy.

A lady of the crew came into the room, Sir, someone wants to talk with you on the phone.

Brian, Wow, it got too late. It's near that Tom will come and ruin everything, including us.

No, sir. The phone is of the organization. They want to know when you will reach.

I will come, tell them in the next half an hour. Well, my Mom, I have to leave you, take very care of yourself. Albert handles everything, and you don't have to worry about anything. I will be back soon.

Elizabeth embraced Brian. She was medium-height and obese, and because Brian was tall, she was standing on her tiptoe. Brian burst into laughter by seeing this scene.

My short and fat Mommy, look, you are standing on your tiptoe.

They both laughed.

In the courtyard of the mansion, the driver with a Mercedes-Benz automobile was waiting for Brian.

Brian said to his mother, So, what's this?

- It will drive you to the organization.

- I don't need it. I will go myself.

Albert, a middle-aged and tall man, had stood by three persons of the crews to see me off. Elizabeth was next to the car. Brian had a look at the white-colored mansion. The building had the same glory of his childhood, with towering poplar trees and the pleasant smell of spring.

He got in the car and drove off. On the way, Tom phoned again.

- Yes, Tom? ...

- Don't come to pick me up. I reached to the organization.

- Okay.

Brian reached to the organization. Two people were waiting in front.

- Hello, Mr. Werner. Everyone is waiting for you. This way, please.

The secretary was sitting in the hall. Brian blinked at her and passed her. The secretary, a young girl, smiled and went to work. Brian entered a room consisting of a row of tables, several chairs, and a large screen. Three people were there; a black-skinned man with white beards and hair and a brown suit, he was Tom. He was in charge of a project that Brian was engaged in it as an astronaut. A young man in a black suit, with a brown leather bag, and a few folders that all of them were on the table. He was Brian's lawyer, Edward. Brian was the sponsor of the project and had to bear all the financial costs. So, he had assigned his lawyer to do the works after his traveling. The third person was a driving force laboratory engineer for a space station, named Reza Ghaffarian.

By having many negotiations with the mentioned people and with several other members of the board of directors of NASA space station, also revising the description and review of operations that were going to do on Mars, then Mr. Ghaffarian explained how to travel and fuel. Later, a person named Marcho took Brian to have the tests and check out the equipment.

Marcho, "Brian, some stuff has been prepared as a gift of the organization for you."

- What are those things? Is it a big cheeseburger?

Marcho Laughed, No. It is a space ecosphere that has growing shrimps, so, you can eat seafood.

- Wow. It is great.

- And, the more exciting of all, which has innovated to protect you against the damages of the Earth's gravity pressure when you are lifting off the planet, is the Antecuarium material, plus the anti-light glasses, special wax, space auto, and memory foam.

- Very good.

- Well, it is better to get ready. Before going, Dr. Angel is going to do a series of tests for you.

- Brian looked at Dr. Angel and smiled, how glad I am that the last woman I see on the Earth is a woman with your beauty.

Marcho whispered in Brian's ear, Brian, she is not eager at all to talk about this matter.

Dr. Angel, thank you, Mr. Werner, please sit in the chair.

Brian raised an eyebrow, With pleasure, Ms. Angel.

With accomplishing tests and wearing clothes, Brian checked the belongings and entered the spacecraft. He looked around and started controlling and coordinating some stuff. A man named Johan, who was in charge of the coordination, accompany Brian to check the impulses and the time of burning fuel by engines. Finally, the shuttle was ready to fly. A few seconds after the launch, Brian shouted for joy.

- Yeah. That is real life.

After launch, Brian was about two days in the Earth orbit and trapped several satellites with the robotic arm of the shuttle and took necessary steps to repair and transport them.

Brian, Susan, beautiful Susan, can you hear me?

The voice on the headphone, Yes, Brian. We have your voice.

- How are you, Susan?

- Fine, what about you? How are things going?

- Great. I feel better when I hear your voice too. So, what is your opinion if you accompany me on the next trip?

- Enough, please. Brian, don't you try to be funny with me.

- I'm serious, everything is excellent here, but without a lady, even the galaxy would be boring for people.

Powell, Brian, let us know when you get into Mars orbit?

- I'm on Mars orbit now.

- But we cannot see you in the picture.

- Don't you have me? But I'm on Mars orbit on my map.

Susan, Brian, here's a problem. We have you in none of the orbits.

Brian calmly, does that mean I'm lost in the galaxy right now?

Tom, Brian, stop joking.

Suddenly the sound was muted.

Brian, Tom, Tom, do you hear me? What happens, oh my God? Brian was staring at the interruption, disconnection, and problems in the deadly silence. So, he got up from the chair and examined the devices. An intense force was pulling the ship inside itself. Brian started recording.

- I'm stuck in an area of space and time. Here the gravity is so high that it does not seem to could run away. The sheer and mysterious darkness that the more it proceeds, the more curious I get. Dear Tom, thank you for letting me experience this beauty. I feel like I'm going into a one-way journey through the depths of a black hole. The spaceship is spinning in a spherical space. Dear Mom, I love you so much. I have experienced everything in this world, and I have no wish except for the love that I have always lacked.

Brian finished his talking and sent his recording to the base station, but he was not sure that Tom and the others would receive the sound. In his cold look, there was a strange fear. The fear was like getting stuck in the middle of the flames of a burning forest. Every moment, the ship was dragged more inside the black hole. He dressed in his clothes and prepared the capsules. He took the necessary supplies and put them near himself. Then, he closed his eyes and leaned against the chair. He remembered a sunny day on the beach with his parents. Brian was an eight-year-old boy at the time. The images of his parents' interactive laughter at the breakfast table, playing and running with his dog, who had killed in a car accident with his father, his father's warm look, and so on emerged. His eyes were closed, but a warm smile had sat on his lips. He heard in his mind, his mother's voice screaming, Brian, my son, slower.

Another memory beside his father's desk.

- When are we going to play golf?

_ Whenever you want. Do you want to go right now?

Albert, But Sir, the lawyers are waiting for you.

- Indeed, nothing and no one is worth it for me to ignore spending time with my son, isn't it, Brian?

- Yes, Dad.

- Remember, in this world, the first thing that is in high priority is only you and your family.

Brian felt a ray of light on his closed eyes. He opened his eyes. In skepticism, he saw a planet facing himself. The spaceship was rapidly moving toward the unknown celestial body. A glimmer of hope shone in Brian's heart. He sat behind the steering chair and took over the handle of the ship. It was getting closer and closer to the planet. He got up, put the oxygen capsule over his shoulder, and grabbed his hat. He took the camcorder, space auto, and the rest of the equipment and placed them next to the oxygen capsule. Brian didn't believe what he saw. The planetoid was in an aura that, after passing through it, Brian felt that the asteroid was very similar to Earth. He was round-eyed with amazement. The ship descended behind a large gate, between the sky and the planet. He put on his hat, picked up his belongings, and left the spaceship. The gate was so high that when Brian raised his head, he couldn't even see the end of the gate. Its material was like gold metal. He knew pushing the door on that greatness was quite useless. But he started pushing on. The door opened without any hassle; there was a road behind the door. But it had an unknown material that didn't look like soil at all. Brian was afraid to move away from the ship. Besides, he could not carry all the oxygen capsules, and it was difficult for him to walk around when he saw the door, fearing that the extraterrestrials might encounter him. Brian was a leap in the dark and passed through the gate. He looked backward and whispered to himself, "Brian, the end of this road is death. So, don't be scared because it won't be any worse. It is your last trip. So, enjoy it."

He got his camera ready and started filming,

- Tom, Although I have no hope of earning this video someday, I have faced the strangest event of my life and started videoing the door. His clothes were more weighty than usual. It was as if the planet had gravity power too, but Brian kept going.

Because of the very similarity of the planet to Earth, Brian decided to do a series of experiments on arrival. First, by examining the planetary weather using an electrochemical Co sensor, Brian found that the air has made from a low percentage of carbon monoxide and, unbelievably, found that half of the air contained oxygen and a significant amount of nitrogen.

Tom, its weather is quite the same as Earth, and it's unbelievable. Maybe, I have landed somewhere on the Earth?

He put the camcorder opposite his face and removed his hat in front of the camcorder.

- As you can see, I can respire easily, as if I were breathing in the pleasure and chilly air by the sea in Greece. However, Greece is not comparable to here. He grabbed the camera and continued on his way, then reached a place just like the plain.

The end of the plain was invisible.

- Wow, what is this?

The boundless beauty of the environment had taken Brian by surprise. The image he saw was just like a sweet dream.

Brian had entered a where that was like a pretty garden. There were of every color of trees; it seemed to have autumn with pleasant weather. The leaves had made a beautiful rainbow. There was a beautiful stream under the shady trees. The flowers in the garden were so beautiful that I could not describe their beauty. Several gold thrones had laid beneath some trees.

Brian, The gold throne?!!! What is this? Am I not really on the Earth's planet? But I've never seen such beauty anywhere on the Earth. Have I died, and here is heaven?

He scratched his hand with the edge of the capsule.

- Alright, it's blood. So, I'm still alive.

He started filming trees and plants.

- See here; Tom, Powell, and Susan. I have encountered a series of plant species that I had never seen on the Earth.

Suddenly, a sound like a parade came to his ears. Where he had stood, he got frozen. In long-distance, several gray-colored three-meter-high shawls were moving in distinct rows. By paying more attention, I realized that there was no creature under them. I got in a fluster, but before I took any action, the shawl-clad beings disappeared.

He took a deep breath. As he swallowed the air in his lungs, a strange euphoria swept through his entire body. Not even his fear of that weird atmosphere did not bother him. The excessive light and shine did not hurt the eyes. The sound of the wind was still impressive as if someone was whispering a pleasant song to its ears. I began to walk in that beautiful garden. A nude creature with a female-look upper body, beautiful face, dragon-like wings, and snake-like scaly lower body was petting a peculiar motioning plant. Brian could not believe what he had seen. So, he lowered his camera, held the breath in his chest, and ran to the other side. After he got away, it was as if Brian had forgotten what he had seen, again he felt the euphoria through his whole body.

He turned back, and saw a water stream, turned on the camera and started to record it.

- And unbelievably, there is a water stream here. Seemingly, it looks like water.

He tasted a little of it.

- Yeah. Indeed, it is water. But how much lighter and tastier it is.

He turned off the camera, took off his clothes, and put them away. He put his feet in the water, experiencing a new feeling that was neither cold nor warm; it was a wonderful feeling. He closed his eyes for a few minutes. In his mind, he was speaking with himself, "What did I truly see? What were they? Where is here? There is no return way. I have gotten close to my death. However, I think even death is worth that I could see a living planet in my life. "

He was in this thought that the sound of the laughter of several people came from afar. He opened his eyes and quickly grabbed his clothes. Surprisingly, he noticed that his body was dry. Regardless, he began to wear his clothes and hid behind a tree which its trunk width was about two meters. The sounds were approaching. Brian was seeking. Suddenly, he sensed a hand on his shoulder. He frightened, and turned back, raised his hand as a sign of submission.

Brian slowly returned with fear. He incredibly saw a woman behind him, "Are you human? Wow, you're a girl."

She was a tall girl with very long hair that almost reached her knees, golden and cascading;

she had a very charming and innocent bony face, a slender nose, and big eyes. Her half-naked body covered by a green dress that was somehow like velvet. But all of the woman's private organs were apparent over the dress, and she was quite like the Earth women. Her legs were bare and slightly larger than usual. Her body shone like a crystal in the glare of the sun.

Brian glanced over at her. The beauty of the girl had made him completely stunned. He admired as he gazed at her, "I had never seen so much beauty gathering in one person. I hope you would be a harmless person as much as your beauty too. Don't understand what I'm saying? Is not it?"

And he added a little body language (gesture of hand and face) to his words, "I...I... got lost. Do you understand? I don't know where I am? Am I on the Earth? Where is here? Where are we now?"

The girl smiled.

- Well, it's a good sign, of course, if the laughing would be pleasant in your land. Look, I'm about putting down whatever I have. I have lost. I only intend to set up my wicked ship and find my way.

What am I saying? You don't understand it.

Girl, Hi, I have never seen you before. Are you alien?

- What? Do you understand my language?

- Yeah, everyone here understands any language. Who are you?

The girl's face was full of calmness.

- I'm Brian Werner. Sorry, I want to know I'm on the Earth or not? If not, I want to know your planet's name? In which galaxy am I? What is your name? And are you a human being or a more complex being?

The girl laughed and invited Brian to sit on the throne. The other girls who were playing and laughing approached and stared at Brian in silence.

Brian, Hi.

Girls at the same time, Hi.

- Welcome our guest and serve him.

- Sit down. I will answer your questions. My name is Mitra, and my planet's name is Pardis. I'm an audition. I know you have a lot of questions but come on, eat something.

- No, thanks. I'm lost.

- You reminded me of someone. From where do you come? Oh my God, you mentioned you came from the Earth, am I right? Are you a human? I thought, why did you remind me of that person? How did you come back? Where's Eve?

- Adam and Eve?!!! How did I come back? Wait. One by one. I am near to have a horn.

- How do you know Adam and Eve?

- Are you Adam?

- No, I'm from Adam's generation, but I'm not him. He has been dead for millions of years.

- Death? What is that?

- It is something strange, so much troubling. First, you tell me what do you mean by what you said?

- Adam and Eve used to live here and were the eyes of God.

- Who's God?

- The king of the Worlds.

- Okay.

- But one day they made a mistake and made God very angry.

- Eating an apple?

- That's right. God got very angry with their deed and banished them to the Earth.

- Just because of eating an apple?

- No, eating an apple was an excuse. Adam and Eve got deported for betraying into the trust of God.

- So, what about Satan? It was he who fooled Adam.

- It has a long story. When we came back home, I will tell you. But you have to know, when God finds out that Adam has feelings which diminish the goodness, God compelled to deport them.

- Forced?

- Yeah, because before that, there was no forgiveness for anyone who disobeyed orders in Pardis, and God forced to banish them despite his interest in them.

- How was their personality?

- Adam and Eve were not like the others. They were greedy and covetous. Maybe the apple was an excuse.

- So, is here heaven?

- Heaven. Yes, right. And you are Adam's son.

- I am of his generation. We are mortal. We experience something called death.

- So, what you mean by dying, inexistence, and capturing the soul is that you perish and annihilate?

- Exactly, and then we are promised to perceive the paradise that is here, Pardis.

Mitra pondered, But it is not right that you don't come back here after God takes your life.

The girls were welcoming and serving Brian. Brian began to eat and drink but discovered new tastes.

- My God, how nice they are. I had never eaten such delicious foods. And he continued,

"Our people think that God is always watching over them, but they don't know that he gave up and punished them for their father's mistake in this way."

- Tell me about the Earth. Is it a scary place?

- I don't know. But it's not like here. Maybe for some, it is a truly terrible place. I have traveled the whole earth. Many people do not have food to eat. They are hungry and thirsty. Many of them are sick, and lots of them are captive by the powers' struggle.

- Whatever you are saying, are they bad things?

- Yes, Mitra. Earth is a truly terrible place. Tell me about God, what does he resemble?

- Do you like to see him?

Brian responded with excitement, Yeah

- Well, then I'll take you to see him.

- Does that mean I can talk to him?

- That is the only hard work in the universe. We see God seldom, just in our prayers, we can meet him. But today is precisely the time to pray. If you want, come with me. If you like I can show you surrounding.

- Yeah. Very good.

- But before that, you have to change your clothes. No one should know where you came from, and you are of Adam's generation.

- Why?

- No one here is breaking the rules. The biggest mistakes here were for Adam and Eve.

After that, some of us decided to help Adam. They sent them some vital things to avoid keeping Adam and Eve in hard situations. When God realized the matter, he dealt with them hard.

- Look. Then, we go and pray for him, good and bad deed. He doesn't pay attention to us at all. He also punishes anyone who helps us.

- Did you say something?

No, it's nothing. Okay, what should I do?

- We go to my house.

- Home? But why there? Persons in your home don't object you for taking me home? How can I say? I mean, when I'm here illegally, isn't it dangerous for me, coming with you?

- The danger? Never. You are safe and secure in my privacy. Here, even God does not attack the privacy of his creatures.

- Do you think we can repair my ship and show me the return way?

- Of course. In Pardis, anyone who needs help will receive assistance. Don't be afraid of it.

Brian was relieved, but he was still dumb and confused.

On the way,

Brian, Are these girls your maids?

- Yes, they are Jinn.

- Has here always such pleasant weather and is pretty?

Mitra wonders, Yeah, was it supposed to be changed?

- Surely not! I was just curious. Why are you helping me? Why don't you entrust me to God!

- I don't know.

- Let me know, are you in two male and female gender too? I mean being a couple and getting married.

- Yes. We are also a kind of human being, and all the behavior you have is truly a legacy that you conveyed from Pardis to the Earth.

- How exciting, did you get married?

- No, the proper time has not yet come. When the suitable time comes, I will marry the man who got chosen by my family.

Brian remembered his mother's words.

- Does that mean the others will choose a spouse for you?

- Yeah.

- So what about yourself? Don't you want your spouse has a particular trait? Or, do you get to fall in love with him?

- Love? What is love? Our all men in this land have several characteristics.

- What does that mean? Does that mean they all have some particular moral attributes? Are they all honest? Are they all wealthy? Are they all handsome?

- Yeah, that's right. Brian, being evil or wicked is nonsense, here.

- What nonsense?

- What is meaningless?
- That there is no difference between humans here. Are you all right persons, have not you experienced the love and the pain of it?
- What is the pain of love?
- I don't know; I haven't experienced it myself.
- What about you? Haven't you got married yet?
- No, I still haven't found anyone I can love her.
- How many people are you on the Earth?
- How many people? Billions.
- Does Billion mean a lot?
- Yes, that means too much, more than you can imagine.

Mitra repeated to herself, More than my imagination.

If you like, we can go home with a chariot.

- A chariot? How excellent, okay.

Mitra read a sentence in a particular voice like a sing, and the chariot as flying at the height of one meter from the surface came towards them. The chariot had no wheel, and no force drove it. It was like a flat board with a handle as a backrest.

Brian, Damn, look at it. Very awesome.

They got on the chariot. Mitra stared at Brian with a smile. Brian, however, was looking around. He felt happy in his inner.

- Mitra, you are taking me home now, what are you saying to your parents about me? They won't ask who I am?

- No, they don't live in my house. I have come to the north to study science. They visit me every day. But they don't stay in my house.

- Do you mean you live alone?

- I am with my maids and my sisters.

- Sister? So we're indeed going to enter heaven. Do they also live here to study?

- Yes.

- Are they okay with this matter?

- Yes, there is nothing wrong with their viewpoint. But my father is one of the scholars of God's court, and he never betrays him. Just enough to hide you from his eyes.

- So, isn't a betrayal whatever you are doing?

Mitra got silent.

- I am eager to see him. I mean, God. You know, I have to say, I believed him, not so much, but well I didn't use to think about him so much. I don't know how to say I didn't think heaven would be a place around here. I thought we have to die and then.

Brian sighed and continued, So we were some extraterrestrials who got banished to Earth. I should have thought about it.

Mitra was silent and stared at him with a smile as if she hadn't understood anything from Brian's words.

They entered Mitra's House. The house was not like the houses on Earth. There was no wall, and the ceiling had mounted on beautiful marble pillars. The cover was like the sky, and a pretty large table surrounded with beautifully decorated chairs was in the middle of the house. Several thrones were scattering around the garden. Beyond the table and in the middle of the pillars, the door frame hung in the air. Mitra indicated that they should go there. There was a large room that had operating screens instead of having walls, with a series of lines like writings steadily moving on them.

- What are these?

- Here is the practice room. We practice here what the professors tell us.

- Have you made it yourself?

- What thing?

- The walls that have these crossing lines look like an LED screen but much more realistic.

No, they originate from the knowledge of God. We don't make anything here. These have existed from eternity.

- Have Adam and Eve also seen such technology?

- Yeah.

- Poor them, how hard the Earth has had for them.

- I have heard they have hurt on Earth.

- How old are you, Mitra?

- Year? What's the year?

- Do you have anything called night and day, or month and year?

- We have the day, but night, no, I don't even know what month or year is.
- Does that mean there is no night after a day here? Don't you sleep and start a new day?
- Yes. We begin every day with the praise of God and rest as the light decreases. But I don't know what you mean by sleep? I think you intend the blessing God gave Adam and Eve.
- Oh, how boring. I can't understand such an amount of comfort. I think it would be tedious after a while. But your possibilities are truly glorious.
- Fatigue and repetition are words used for a mortal thing. These words do not make sense here. Brian, time here is not in the sense that you have experienced.
- My brain is near to get hung. It would be better, not more concentrated on our differences.
- So let's go to the music room.
- Let's go.
They left the place through another door. They entered a room that looked like a flower-filled plain. The girls were playing music with strange instruments. The sounds were so sweet as if it polished the soul.
- I feel fresh. Are these girls your sisters?
- No, they are maids.
- How beautifully they play.
- Yeah. It is so sweet.

- Are there such facilities in every home?

- Yes.

- They are all beautiful but not as much of your beauty.

Mitra was amazed at the praise that Brian gave her. A strange feeling was about to create in her inner.

- Don't you want to introduce me to your family?

- Yes, probably everyone is doing something.

How many sisters do you have?

- Three sisters and two brothers.

- So you also have brothers. Do they live with you?

- No, my brothers are the southern gatekeepers. They have crucial jobs, and they are not usually here.

- Have they gotten married?

- One of them has gotten married, and the other will get married soon. Let me cry out the girls. But before, we have to go into the dressing room to change your clothes.

Mitra directed Brian to the dressing room. She summoned the maids.

- Pomona, bring the proper costume for the gentleman.

Pomona saluted as a sign of approval and went toward the walls and brought a costume for Brian. When the clothes handed over to Brian, he felt no weight.

- Is the stuff of this outfit silk?

- No, these clothes have made of light.

The light? All right. So I better not ask too much.

Brian put on the clothes. The costume was half-naked. It was like a cloak that stretched down to his knees. The clothes were indigo in color.

- Why are most of you wearing green clothes? Green in different tonalities?

It is the most popular color in our land, maybe because of its benefits.

- Have all the clothes here made of light?

- No, we also have Sondus (thin and delicate silk), Istabraq (thick silk), Dibaj (a kind of silk), and Harir (ultra-thin silk) clothes here.

- But these clothes do not cover any part of the body. Look, my private organ is visible. Why are you wearing them? Although I am a man, I am not comfortable in these clothes.

- These clothes are decorative.

- But won't your men and women feel bad seeing the other one's naked body? I don't know, I mean, lust sense or whatever else. Showing our private organs to others on earth would be great immorality.

- The private parts? Lust? It is as if Adam and Eve have built new customs! Everyone here has everything and everyone he/she wants.

- Does that mean you have sex with someone until now?

- Of course, I have had.

- That is, well. So, residents of paradise are not as much stupid as I thought.

- Okay, who were they?
- Frequently, it was too much. Before marriage, we can have sex with anyone we desire.
- How frankly you are talking about this matter. I thought you were shyer.

Mitra was round-eyed.

Brian, Excuse me. I did not pay enough consideration. You probably don't even know the meaning of embarrassment.

And whispered to himself,

One of the reasons it is named paradise is this.

Mitra directed Brian to the mirror hall. The room on the four sides had covered with mirrors instead of walls.

- Oh, my God. I had never seen such great mirrors. Which material have these mirrors made?
- Salt.
- Very exciting.

A maid brought a drink for Brian.

- I wouldn't like it. Thank you.
- Why?
- I'm afraid to overdrink.
- I'm sure you still want to ask, but eating and drinking here make no problem.

Mitra sat down, and one maid began to comb her hair. Brian was all eyes when he watched Mitra.

- What are you watching?

- You, so much pretty. Your hair, your eyes, your lips, all of them flare up me entirely.

- What beautiful words.

- These words are you. By the way, will you have any relationship with anyone else you love after marriage?

- No, God only keeps us for the one person who we will form a family after we marry him.

- Why do you call your sisters? How do we have to find them in such a big house? Are the houses here as big as this one?

- Yeah, there are seventy thousand palaces here, each of which has seventy thousand rooms.

- Look. Then my mom says our house is big. Come on. If you come to Earth, you will be utterly upset.

Mitra stared at Brian.

- Aha. Yes, you don't know the meaning of being upset.

Two maids came forward to open the door on the left side of the mirror hall. Mitra guided Brian and crossed through the tunnel covered with green leaves and white flowers and reached the first room again. Three beautiful girls were standing next to each other and watching Brian with a smile. Brian whistled and was stunned.

- Oh, my God. What's going on here? What beautiful ladies!

The girls said hello.

Mitra, Girls, this is Brian. Brian, these are my sisters, Uros, Aphrodite, and Anahita.

Uros had black hair and big black eyes full lips and olive skin. But Aphrodite had wheat-colored hair and sea-colored eyes, Anahita by having hazel-colored eyes and curly hair was more than the other resembled Mitra. Each of them gave the meaning to the boundless beauty.

Their bodies were like a crystal as if they had exposed their bones because of having excessive transparency. And the garments had made the beauty of their bodies hundredfold. Each one's clothes were one of the colors of the rainbow that seemed to wrap around them like ultra-thin silk (Harir).

Their shoes were made of gold and adorned with other jewelry like pearls, and the strap was red ruby. All of their bodies were obvious. And Brian, who had never seen such beauty in any of the women on earth, was all eyes.

- Nice to meet you, ladies.

Uros, So do we. I've never seen you before.

Aphrodite, Are you a friend of Mitra?

Anahita, No, Mitra didn't have such a friend. I didn't see anyone like you neither in the northland nor in southland. You have to come from the west or the east because I haven't traveled there yet.

Aphrodite, That's right. She has just matured and has not been able to travel to many places yet.

Uros, Anahita is our youngest sister. The oldest one is Aphrodite, who is going to marry the son of one of the clans of Light House Paradise, then is Mitra, and at last, me.

- Mitra, Girls, wait. Why are you talking so fast? I will tell you everything. First, let's take our guests to rest in the garden. The girls laid Brian on a throne, and they sat around him, and immediately maids began to serve food for him. Two maidservants came to play music, and several good-looking of them began to dance. The girls treated him as if he had been living there for many years.

Brian, I'm lucky, even when I'm lost.

Mitra began to describe the event. Anahita did not know Adam and Eve, but Uros and Aphrodite knew everything.

Brian, I want to know everything about Adam and Eve and their fate.

Anahita, Well, let's go to the memories room.

Uros, Anahita, wait; First, we talk about his presence here and then go wherever you say.

Mitra, Our daddy shouldn't know anything about this matter.

Anahita, Why?

- Because in that case, daddy would hand him over to God, and God would punish him.

Uros, Let us know, from which door you came in? Where was the guard?

Brian, From an ultra-big golden door, I didn't see any guards there. The first person I saw was Mitra.

Aphrodite (addressed Uros), He has entered from the Eternal Paradise's door.

Brian, how many doors does the paradise have? Why are there so many large gates? Nobody knows where you are.

The girls laughed.

Anahita, Baby, no one knows where you are, not us.

Mitra, Heaven has eight clans, and consequently, eight doors. The first door is the entrance of Blessing Heaven. The second door for Barin Heaven (topmost), the third one is for Comfort Paradise, and the fourth door, from which you entered, is for Eternal Heaven. The fifth one is for Resort Paradise, which we call it the ultimate residence. The sixth door is for Ferdows Paradise (the best place in heaven), the seventh one is for Health House, and the latest door is for Light House.

Aphrodite, Of course, what Mitra said is not the name of doors, but the names of the different heavenly clans, each have an entrance.

Brian, I understood. On Earth, we also have such divisions as this.

Aphrodite, does this mean that the children of Adam have raised so much that they have become clans?

Brian, Yes, I think we are about 196 clans or countries.

Anahita (surprisingly), What? I thought Earth is a too small and negligible place.

Brian, No, it's not. We built the world with our hard work. We have experienced things that you do not even know what it means, and in my opinion, life without them is meaningless.

Uros, what are these?

Brian, Sadness, fear, stress, hunger, hope, love, crying, without them, what happiness can mean. We worked hard to build our world, and I think despite all the shortcomings, it's still a beautiful world.

The girls looked at Brian in surprise, and the words Brian said were meaningless for them. Brian continued,

- See, you don't understand the meaning of the better word at all because all your days and moments are good, so you don't have the better ones. You don't be sad to enjoy double happiness after that. Give it up. Let's get out of this discussion and enjoy the space.

Aphrodite, we don't know the meaning of the words you say because we have not experienced such states for those words to happen to us. Maybe someday, if we are in your situation, we will understand the suffering of those words.

Uros, we will never be in a sorry state because of God's kindness.

Aphrodite, Of course, our fathers also suffered greatly when the accursed Satan was the king of Pardis. We had not created at that time, and for that reason, we are in prosperity and comfort.

Brian shook his head at the sign of understanding and started drinking. The children were busy and happy. Mitra was different for Brian and made Brian ecstatically happy.

Anahita, Come on, guys. Let's go to the memories room.

Aphrodite, Anahita, your curiosity sense is commendable.
Brian laughed.

Mitra, she is right. We should go. We have a lot of fun.

Brian and the girls got up from the throne and went to the entrance door. The door opened, and they entered an area that was very much like a football field. The stairs had surrounded the space that was transparent and luminous jelly.

Mitra, Come here, Brian.

Brian, Where's here anymore?

Uros, this is the memories room. When the memories uttered, you can see the origin of those memories here.

- Wow, my God! It is pretty awesome. Tell me (addressed Mitra), if someone lies what will happen, will the reality of the memory still be exposed?

Anahita, What's the lie?

Brian, Lie. A word is against the truth.

Aphrodite laughed, no one is lying here, Brian.

Brian clapped and sat on the chair, "Well, let's sit down and tell me the memories. So, which one of you like to start?"

Mitra, Aphrodite, you should start.

Anahita, Wow, I'm so excited.

Aphrodite caressed Anahita's hair with a smile and began to utter. When she triggered to explain, the space became thoroughly dark, and a four-dimensional visual area formed like the theater scene. But the visual image was like a dream and blurrier than reality. We were all silent and staring at the floor.

Aphrodite, the memory I want to tell you goes back a long way to the pre-creation of Adam.

With each sentence of Aphrodite, images were forming and eventually were disappearing into a mist.

Before the creation of Adam, God had created other beings, and they lived in Pardis. God granted everyone a position according to their aptitude and worth. Jinns are of the most inferior races in Pardis because of the type of creation and their element of existence, and therefore the positions they hold in Pardis are worthless. But among all, there was a jinni, named Satan. He was able to prove himself to God with a lot of hard work and effort as far as he became one of the elders of the court and attained high rank. Whenever God went out of Pardis for a short period to have a new creation, despite all the servants and angels, God identified Satan as his successor, and that was an unattainable position for a jinni. One day, God went out of Pardis to create new beings, and shortly afterward, he returned with his new creatures, two brothers named Angra Minio and Hormazd. God created them to be God's right and left hand. But all along, he realized their differences. Hormazd was wise, thoughtful, honest, and kind, but Angra Minio was egocentric and selfish. His deeds and decisions were momentary and thoughtless. God commissioned the angels to train them.

Perversely, Satan taught to Angra Minio, and it didn't take a long time for Angra Minio to become the dependent and disciple of Satan.

Brian, how much they suited to each other.

Aphrodite, If there was a monster inside Angra Minio, it was definitely in a deep sleep, Brian. That was Satan, who awoke it.

Brian, please go on, Aphrodite.

In Pardis lived a gorgeous girl named Sependarmaz. A beautiful, wise girl who until then had not allowed any man to take advantage of her.

She relied on that only one man could court her, a man who had better makings than others.

Hormuzd and Angra Mainyu both were in love with Sependarmaz unbeknownst to each other, and they took their appeal to Izad [God]. Izad summoned Sependarmaz and asked her to adopt for herself and choose one of the two brothers.

Sependarmaz arranged a race so that she could cherry-pick the one who was qualified. In all rivalries, Angra Mainyu overwhelmed Hormuzd fraudulently and won the races, but contrary to his expectations, Sependarmaz chose Hormuzd as her spouse. Angra Mainyu appealed to Izad but Izad overruled the objection and said, "I left the decision making to Sependarmaz. If you have any objection, you must tell her because the justice between you two is a matter that is in the hands and heart of Sependarmaz."

Angra Mainyu blamed Sependarmaz in front of the crowd and made her very upset, "O' Sependarmaz, you cannot snub the upshot of the race and if so, you have wronged me and are in breach of the promise you made before. You should know that no one before you did such a thing in Pardis."

Brian and the rest watched every moment of the dispute.

Sependarmaz said, "Angra Mainyu, my marriage verdict was not based on winning the race, but the way the contestants behaved. There is something wrong with you but there is goodness in Hormuzd's soul. I noticed that by every imaginable trick you pushed Hormuzd aside but Hormuzd was silent because of a sense of brotherhood."

Hormuzd patiently advised Angra Mainyu to calm down, but Angra Mainyu angrily pushed him away.

"It is a lie that you have made up to hide the injustice you have done to me. From today, I contemplate you and Hormuzd more hostile to me than any other enemy," said Angra Mainyu to Sependarmaz.

Hormuzd's heart broke by this proclamation, and he refrained from marrying Sependarmaz and went after his brother. Angra Mainyu had gone into a cave and was crying bitterly.

Hormuzd entered and slowly sat next to him, "Brother, I don't want to be your enemy. You are all of my possession, I get complimented with you. I forgot about marrying Sependarmaz. You can marry her."

Angra Mainyu got excited and went out of the cave in utter selfishness, unsympathetic to Hormuzd's feelings, and went to Sependarmaz and discussed the matter with her. As soon as Sependarmaz realized Hormuzd's intentions, she fell for him even more and once again rejected Angra Mainyu. Days passed and Hormuzd avoided Sependarmaz during that time.

One night, Izad went to Spendarmaz's house and asked her about the status quo and found out about the two brothers' feelings and intentions. But he allowed the passage of time to bring everything back to normal.

For a long time, there was no sign of Izad. Everyone knew that when Izad was not in Pardis, it was creating a new creature in the heavens, but this time its absence was longer than usual. Izad spent days on a row, alone in its loneliness, fascinated and mesmerized by the creature that it was creating. Everyone was waiting to see the creature. Meanwhile, Iblis [Satan] was pissed off because the new creature had secured a special place in Izad's heart.

The guys were staring at the theatre stage as the scene turned gray.

Aphrodite continued, "The epoch turned dark. Iblis, Izad's substitute, had become cruel and wicked in his absence, and while Izad had forsaken Paradise in its loneliness, Iblis mistreated the Pardis people and had a special agent to do so."

Brian, "One can guess who it was."

Aphrodite, "Yes, and the first person who went to meet it was Sependarmaz. Angra Mainyu went to Spendarmaz's house with a group of jinn and asked her to submit to his desire. When Sependarmaz refused, the jinn chained her up and Angra Mainyu was resorting to force but Hormuzd and the court guards arrived and a fierce fight broke out between the two brothers and Hormuzd won.

Angra Mainyu, who was defeated by Hormuzd, angrily left Spendarmaz's house in fear. Hormuzd slowly released the girl's hands and said, "I'm sorry . . . Angra Mainyu did this . . . this . . ."

"Don't say anything, just hug me. Stay with me tonight, Hormuzd," pleaded Sependarmaz.

Hormuzd asked the guards to watch over Pardis. He softly hugged Sependarmaz and put his hand on her legs and arms and lifted her up and put her on the bed. He knelt beside the bed and stared into her face as tears slowly ran down Spendarmaz's eyes. Hormuzd did not know what was dripping down Spendarmaz's eyes, but he felt great grief upon seeing it.

Aphrodite was silent. The scene was going on.

Hormuzd, "What should I do in this situation?"

- "Hug me, Hormuzd. I'm at your disposal."

Hormuzd stripped Sependarmaz of her clothes, caressed her body by his hand, and slowly closed her eyes, "You are like light. Like a breeze."

He kissed her eyes and then her lips. Flames of love burned his body. He pulled Spendarmaz's black long hair away from her body and boobs and mingled his body and soul with Spendarmaz's body and soul and they began making love.

Brian was too shy to watch the scene and said, "I think it was a series of private memories between them, wasn't it? It is not right to go so deep into their private life."

"Whatever it is, it is very handsome. I have never seen such passion nearby," commented Mitra.

Brian said, "You are beautiful too . . . it is stunning because it is with love."

"What is love?" asked Anahita.

Brian, "Love is what makes a person in the world inversely from everyone else, more beautiful and sweetest of all. Love means that from the moment you feel he is different, you rip your heart out of your chest and hand it over to him and thereafter, you live in his hands."

Mitra, "That is great."

Eros, "That's black if you want to live for someone else."

Brian, "I think you are both right. Love can be black or great. It depends on how we look at it."

Aphrodite said, "Well, let's continue. The next day, Hormuzd and Sependarmaz publicly announced their marriage, and that angered Angra Mainyu more than before.

Fear and darkness had swept across Pardis. It was a dark age. All science houses were under Iblis' control. The jinn had become rulers of Pardis, the same ones who were serving men and audits and the angels and Hormuzd did their best to protect the treasures of science and creatures of Pardis. A long-time passed and in the absence of Izad,

Hormuzd and Sependarmaz had two children, Vio and Tishtria . . .

Eros, "Our grandfathers . . ."

Brian, "Your grandfathers?"

Mitra, "Yeah . . . Vio was the father of my father, Amortat; and Tishtria was the father of my mother, Mehraveh."

Brian, "Let's see, you said you are immortal, right?"

Mitra, "That's right."

- "So Hormuzd, Sependarmaz, Angra Mainyu and all of them must be alive."

Anahita, "Certainly they are alive. Hormuzd is the god of war and the commander of the Pardis Corps."

Eros, "However, Hormuzd and Sependarmaz had five other children later, each of those seven children is now a god at Izad's court, controlling the rest of the planets and help Izad to lead the world."

Brian, "So, what is their name?"

Eros, "Wait a moment. I will show you our family tree."

Eros waved his hand in the air. A screen appeared and images appeared on the screen, "These that you saw are Hormuzd and Sependarmaz.

"The first child, Vio, the wind god, had three children named Sepanteh Armitee, Hiorotat, and Amortat.

"The second child, Tishtria, the rain god and his children, my mother Mehraveh and Apam Napat.

"The third child, Atr, the fire god, and his only child, Indra.

"The fourth, Varthanya, the god of victory and his child Anu.

"The fifth, Heomah, the god of health who had three children named Asha, Humaneh, and Azar.

"The sixth child, Sur, god of celebration and feast and his only child, Boq.

"The last child, Hormuzd, and his only daughter Nahid, goddess of light and her children Tir and Oshbam."

Brian, "How many children does Angra Mainyu have?"

Aphrodite said, "Be patient and listen to the rest of the story, Adam's son," and continued, "The Iblis' wickedness continued until one day suddenly Izad came to Pardis from the heavens and the light returned to Pardis as soon as he arrived."

Brian, "Why in these memories, Izad is seemingly inside a cloud, and his face and voice is not clear?"

Anahita, "Inside a cloud? That's not true. We see and hear his image and voice clearly."

Mitra, "Maybe because you have no perception of Izad. Anyways, you are a mortal being, so your eyes, ears, and mind are closed."

Brian thought a moment and nodded.

Aphrodite, "Izad called everyone to his court to know about Pardis conditions; and in love with, and intoxicated by his new creature, began to speak, "Today you all have come here to see my best creature. As of now, he is a part of me in Pardis. I called him Adam and blew my breath in him. He is above all of you. From today, Adam will be my successor and heir to Pardis."

Adam stood there magnificently.

"Prostrate to Adam," said Izad with a loud voice.

Everyone prostrated and Adam calmly stared at them. Without bowing his head, Iblis went up the stairs of the stage, walked around Adam and looked at him up and down, then angrily gazed at Izad and said, "How on earth do you ask us to prostrate to this creature? Why do you think he is better than us and your successor? Do you mean you have forgotten all our efforts and worship and promoted this creature to this status overnight?"

Izad, "Iblis, are you disobeying me?"

- "Excuse me, Izad. but I will never agree to take this creature as your heir and I will never comply with him."

Izad, "Go away, Iblis, and think well about what you said, you are disobeying me."

Iblis furiously got out of the court.

Brian, "I am losing my fortitude. Why can't I see Izad's image?"

Mitra held Brian's hands, "No problem. Maybe you can see it with your mortal eyes when you get close to it."

Brian smiled.

Aphrodite, "The angels and courtiers explained the event, and Iblis was informed of Iblis' betrayal and ordered to arrest Iblis and its followers."

The angels apprehended them and brought them to the court. Izad was seated on its throne with utmost glory and calmly watched as they entered. Adam was not there. The angels entered, and behind them, Iblis and Angra Mainyu with the gang of sinful jinn entered, their hands were tied with ropes of light beams. All were walking in the hallway and the sound of their footsteps filled the entire space until they reached Izad's throne and stopped.

Izad cast a glance at Iblis like a wise man looks at an idiot and said with a powerful voice, "Gabriel . . . say it . . ."

Eros softly whispered in Brian's ear in a way not to distract the others, "Gabriel is an intimate and trustworthy angel of Izad."

Brian nodded to show he understands.

Gabriel, "Today, Iblis has been summoned here for betraying the status given to him by Izad and because of harassing Pardis' creatures."

Izad, "Iblis, you may state your defense, if you like."

Iblis glanced at Izad, love, and anger filled its eyes, and he said, "I shield myself . . . Izad, have I been a bad servant for you so far?"

Izad, "It is not a good excuse for what you did. State the grounds for your misdemeanor."

- "Tell me Izad, where were you when I did all that? You left us alone and went away. I just established order in Pardis based on my own method."

Izad, "What is all the rage for, Iblis?"

Iblis laughed, "Rage!!! You finally got it. You preferred a creature that you didn't test to us and left us to our own devices for a long time for his sake. And what happened when you came back? Tell me what happened? I will never prefer him to you and if you give me time, I will prove he is not worthy of all this attention and status."

Izad glanced at Gabriel and turned to the courtiers who stood with bowed heads and said loudly, "I, your Izad, the Lord of beings, at this moment permanently deport Satan and his corps from Paradise to the Black Planet. They have no right to return again."

Iblis, "I object your honor, that means the achievement of all of these services goes out of the window so easily because of a blunder?"

Izad, "Ask me for something in return for the services you rendered."

- "Please do not make us mortal after our deportation from Paradise and agree on me to show you the true nature of man."

Aphrodite, "Izad thought that Iblis would beg for forgiveness, but when Iblis stated the relief he sought, Izad became more and more desperate, "Take them out . . ."

Hormuzd shouted with a loud voice, "Izad, please be lenient to Angra Mainyu, he was a stooge of Iblis and under its command. Please spare him."

Angra Mainyu raised his head and shouted crossly, "I don't need you to defend me. I am the commander of the Iblis Corps and remain loyal to him forever."

Hormuzd, "No, Angra Mainyu. You say this because you are angry . . ."

Angra Mainyu laughed, "It am not so, Bro. I'm your sole enemy from now on."

Izad turned to Iblis and Angra Mainyu and said, "Tell me since when you could have become so bad?"

Iblis, "You will find that in our situation, Adam will be worse off than us, and if you don't want your righteousness to be questionable, set some restrictions for Adam to see how much he sticks to your commands."

"Izad, I think Iblis is right in this part. If you do so, you will not leave any room for objection," said one of the courtiers.

Eros got up, "Well, you know the rest."

Brian, "Yeah. It was the apple tree restriction and the rest is history."

Brian yawned. His eyelids felt heavy.

Brian, "Tell me Mitra, will I own one of those seventy thousand rooms?"

Mitra, "Of course, why not . . ."

- "I'm so tired. But we don't rest like you, we sleep . . ."

- "Yeah, you said that before. How do you like your room to be?"

- "It must have four walls so that no one enters without my permission. A bed to sleep, a full-length mirror."

Mitra replied, "Okay, I will tell them to arrange it for you," then she called the maids and explained to them.

Eros asked Mitra about sleep and Mitra explained it.

Eros, "So we shouldn't wake you up until you want to."

Brian, "I will be grateful if you don't."

After a few minutes, the maids returned. Brian and Mitra got up.

Anahita, "When you wake up, we all go for a walk around the town."

Brian, "Great."

Aphrodite, "Are you okay we throw a party to get Brian meet our friends?"

Mitra said, "Guys, Brian should go get some rest. We will talk about it when he wakes up," and took Brian to his room.

The room was very interesting. Every brick was made of gold or silver and the walls smelled good. There was only a bed and a mirror in the room.

Mitra, "Do you like your room?"

- "Yeah, but it was better if there were a window and two chairs at this corner and a toilet."

Mitra, "I will tell them to arrange that for you . . . my goodness, we don't have toilets here."

- "Excuse me ma'am, but how do you relieve yourself?"

- "By sweating . . ."

- "Oh my god . . . I don't fathom . . . "

- "Here, 99.5% of the foodstuff is absorbed in the body and the rest is excreted by sweating."

- "Is it because of your metabolism or foodstuff?"

- "Foodstuff."

- "Well, then I guess I don't need it either."

- "But I tell them to put a bathroom in your room."

- "If there is a wardrobe to keep my clothes in it, it would be much better. I probably miss the whole day just because I have to find the dressing room . . . Well, how long does it take to do all that I asked?"

- "Right now . . ."

Mitra called the maids and in the blink of an eye, all the facilities she requested were provided.

Mitra, "What do you like to see through the window? A plain, a desert or a forest?"

- "A forest . . ."

Mitra went to the left wall of the room and with her hand, drew a circle six feet wide and the circle turned into a window.

- "Do you mind if it has a silk curtain . . ."

- "Sure . . ."

The maids installed white silk curtains over the window panes.

Brian placed his backpack and other junk on the table.

Mitra, "Do you need something?"

- "No, thank you . . . just to wake up in my own bed and all of this turn out to be a dream."

Mitra smiled and went out.

Brian lay on the bed . . . as if he was lying on the clouds. He fell asleep in the blinking of an eye. In a dream, he saw his mother calling him with open arms.

- "Brian . . . my son . . . come here. I need you so much."

His dream was dark and cold.

Brian hugged his mother . . .

- "I will be back, mom . . . I will be back no matter what."

He half-opened his eyelids and fell asleep again.

It took a long time for him to wake up. Brian woke up and sat on his bed. He looked around and shouted loudly.

- "No . . . no . . . this damned thing is not a dream . . . I am stuck in Paradise."

Anahita hurried into the room and said cold-bloodedly, "If you need anything, you can ring that doorbell at the corner."

Brian desperately dropped his head, "Okay, thank you."

Anahita sat on the bed next to Brian . . .

Brian, "Would you please fetch me a glass of water."

- "By all means . . . here, drink . . ."

- "Where is Mitra?"

- "Worshiping with the rest . . ."

- "What? Why didn't she tell me? I wanted to see the Lord."

- "You asked yourself not to wake you up. They will be back at any time. They asked me to stay home so that nobody finds out about you."

- "Thank you . . ."

- "I have to find a way to get back to Earth . . ."

- "Only the Grand Master can help you . . ."

- "Who is he?"

- "He is the one who knows all the sciences . . . however, he is very close to Izad."

- "So, that means we have to ask him very indirectly."

- "Aphrodite is a pupil of the Grand Master and incidentally, she is one of Master's favorite students. If you like, we can take action through her."

- "Yeah, that's a good idea."

Enter the maid,

- "The ladies are waiting for you in the consultation hall."

Brian, "But how should we find it?"

Anahita laughed, "You don't look for it. When you open the door, just think about entering the consultation hall, then the door will open toward it."

Brian did so and when he opened the door, he saw a large circular table in the middle of the room with Mitra and her sisters sitting around it.

Brian, "Hi, girls, how are you? You didn't tell me you were going to see Izad so soon."

Eros, "You said yourself not to wake you up."

- "Yeah, but I didn't know what time had you chosen to pray."

Mitra smiled, "Come sit down, while you were asleep we began to think and made some decisions."

Brian, "Okay, so you can do some useful work, huh . . ."

The girls gazed at Brian.

Brian, "Just a joke . . . forget it . . . go ahead, Mitra."

Aphrodite, "If you stay here, we can arrange so that no one finds out you are of the human race . . ."

Brian, "I don't want to stay here. I want to go back to Earth. Before you arrive, I told the same to Anahita that I must go back, but I have a few things to do before that."

Mitra, "What are those things?"

- "First, I have to meet Izad . . . But in a way so that I quickly get out of here afterward. Secondly, I have to take away some samples and videos from here."

Mitra glanced at Brian, ((Don't go . . . you mean Earth is better than here?))

- "I have people waiting for me there. Life without them makes no sense to me. I'm not used to this lifestyle."

Eros glanced at Mitra and then said to Brian, "If you feel like, get prepared to go out and walk around the city together . . ."

Brian, "Yeah, good idea. Wait, I go and get my camera."

Aphrodite, "Moreover, some of our friends will come here tonight . . ."

Brian asked as he walked toward the door, ((How should I introduce myself?))

Aphrodite said with a surprised voice, "Well, you are Brian, aren't you? who are you supposed to be?"

- "See, don't they ask who you are and where did you come from?"

- "No, why should they ask? They will know as much about you as you like to tell them."

- "That's good. I go get ready."

Eros, "Mitra . . . baby . . . do you have a bad feeling?"

Mitra, "Eros, he is so different . . . I hope he doesn't go . . ."

Anahita, "He is not fruit and beverages, is he?"

The girls looked at Anahita, "What's it? We only like fruits and beverages or other stuff like that . . . and we wish they are there . . ."

The girls ignored Anahita's words.

Aphrodite, "Call Pomona and tell her to tell our friends."

Eros, "Okay . . ."

In downtown,

Mitra and Brian were a few steps ahead, and Aphrodite and Eros were walking behind them. Anahita was toying with Brian's backpack.

Brian, "Thank goodness. Finally, I saw some men among all these nymphs and fairies."

The street was wide and spacious. Both sides of the street were decorated with beautiful but strange trees.

Brian, "Mitra, tell me what is the name of these trees? How beautiful they are."

Mitra, "This tree is called Tuba. It has any fruit you imagine. Very yummy and great. I love these fruits so much."

People were passing by and the jinn was selling goods . . . At the end of the street was a big square. The city marketplace was around the square and tents were set up. When Brian got into one of them, he encountered a strange scene. The tents were very large for their appearance, such that their end was out of sight. He took the camera from Anahita and started filming. He realized that he was not attracting any attention. Nobody noticed anyone else there.

Brian, "Guys, tell me what is your source of income? I mean, what do you give to the seller in exchange for buying these things?"

Eros, "We don't give anything ... Izad provides us with them and the jinn supply it to the market . . ."

- "Interesting, Izad is very generous to you. Well, the next question is why is the light dimming?"

Eros, "Because it's late at night and people must rest . . ."

- "Oh, so this is the color of your nights . . . like a sunrise . . . beautiful."

Behind the tents was another street with castles similar to Mitra's mansion. There were beds in front of the doors and men and women were dancing and celebrating. Happy children ran around among the crowd. Almost every thousand feet, music bands were playing and dancers were dancing. The dancers' appearance was interesting to Brian. It was as if their bodies were fluorescent. They looked like women, but a tad smaller.

- "Mitra, who are these guys? Are they human?"

- "No, these are fairies. They play and dance for men and serve them."

While they talked, a child collided hard with Brian's leg. Brian bent over, he was a little boy.

Brian, "Are you okay?"

Child, "What?"

Mitra said, "Go on playing . . . Brian, we are immortal. We read about something called pain only in the treasure chest of science, as we have nothing called sadness or sleep or even love," her voice was shaking as she said the word *love*.

Brian, "Mitra, are you okay? I feel you are very depressed . . . can I help you?"

Mitra, "Since I met you, I feel like someone has placed his foot on my heart and pushes hard. You are so different Brian . . . I can't explain it to you because I myself don't know anything more."

Brian stared into Mitra's eyes and gently kissed her lips. No one but Anahita noticed them. Everyone was dancing.

Brian looked at Mitra, "Could you find an explanation for it?"

Mitra smiled.

Anahita jumped into the discussion, "It's better to do this out of Eros's sight. He doesn't like Brian too much."

Brian, "Thanks for your tip, Anahita."

Then he turned to Mitra, "Come to my room tonight to be together. After the party . . . okay?"

Mitra, "Okay. Brian. Today for the first time, I was not mindful of prayer. I was thinking of you all thc time."

It was unclear what Brian's feeling was and to what extent. But Mitra was feeling strange.

The jinn carried trays of drink and food among the people and everybody ate and drank. No one cursed or pulled a prank. Everyone was minding his or her own business. Everyone spoke kindly to each other and were happy to meet one another. But Brian was immersed in himself. He was thinking of meeting Izad by any means possible and ask him questions. The thought of visiting Izad had taken over Brian's mind. It was as if he was angry with Izad. He was into himself as Aphrodite called him. In every corner, people were having fun and making love but no one except Brian was looking at others . . .

- "Brian, it's time to go. The guests will arrive soon . . ."

Brian smiled at Mitra, "Okay, let's go . . ."

As they walked in the passageway, a giant bird attracted Brian's attention. It had a bird head with feathers on its body with large wings and a height of about ten feet. Brian was thrilled to see that creature and approached it.

Brian, "Oh my gosh, what's this?"

Aphrodite grabbed Brian's hands and took him to a corner. The girls walked quickly behind them as well.

Aphrodite said angrily, "What are you doing? It is true that creatures in Pardis are not curious, but they are not stupid either. Don't you think a creature that is very similar to a human being and is curious about one of our creatures, doesn't get their attention?"

Brian, "You are right, Aphrodite. I will be more careful from now on."

While they were talking, an army entered the passageway. The jinn and fairies and other creatures bowed and humans stopped moving as a sign of respect and cleared the path. The soldiers' appearance was strange to Brian. They were tall and had canes taller than themselves, and they wore tall green robes so that their faces were not recognizable.

On a large chariot that floated in the air, a creature was moving with a human body and eagle's wings. It was tall, with a robust, masculine body without any clothes but it had no genitals either. It was handsome and charismatic. The soldiers marched at the front and back of the chariot in regular rows, but the man on chariot suddenly ordered them to stop.

"My goodness, it found out," whispered Eros, "It sensed the presence."

Brian, "What are you talking about?"

Mitra, "Calm down. Brian, don't look at its face under any circumstances and stand behind us."

Brian, "Will someone explain to me what is it?"

Anahita, "It is Azrael [death angel], a senior angel. It is the one that catches the soul and returns the soul of Adam and his children to Izad."

Brian, "What? Azrael?"

Mitra, "Yes, and now it has sensed that you are here because it is dealing with you mortal beings all the time."

Azrael got down the chariot and began to walk among the crowd.

Eros, "Close your eyes and don't look at it when it says hello."

Azrael, "Hello to you . . ."

The crowd said hello in response.

Anahita, "Wow, how lovely it is."

The group looked at her and Anahita stared ahead.

Azrael asked the jinn and fairies to raise their bowed heads.

Brian and the girls slowly backed away and got out of the crowd and ran home. Azrael looked around and boarded the chariot and the people also dispersed.

The guys stopped running in another street. Brian noticed that despite running a long distance, he did not feel tired or short of breath at all.

Brian, "God save us, please someone tell me what is going on here? Why did we run away?"

Mitra, "If Azrael found you, it would take you directly to Izad, either along with your body or just your soul. Secondly, you are a mortal, Brian. Your soul could be snatched by looking at its face."

Brian, "That means I would die."

Eros, "That is right, and you could never go back to Earth or stay here."

Brian was scared. He puffed his chest and said, "It's better to go back home as soon as possible because I don't want to die here."

Mitra smiled and grabbed his hands. Brian felt comfortable. He threw his arms around Aphrodite and Mitra's shoulders, "Thank god you are here. If you were not here, it would be worse than hell. It is allegedly Paradise, but every moment is full of fear."

A pleasant sound of singing filled the sky, and everyone was delighted by listening to it.

Brian said to Mitra, "The birds here sing great."

Mitra, "It is not a bird; it is the lady singer."

- "Lady singer? What the hell is that?"

- "She is coming our way and you will see her."

Anahita, "We have not heard her voice for quite a while."

A woman with a human head and long ears, a sparrow-like face and a body like a marten but larger showed up.

Anahita, "Hi, lady dancer."

- "Hello guys, my heart is filled with joy by seeing you again."

Aphrodite, "Our hearts too, by your singing . . ."

- "Thanks, it was a long time that I had not sung. That is because I traveled to a distant planet and met Davaalpaa there."

Eros, "Oh, it is not difficult to guess what happened."

Lady singer, "That is right, Eros. It was very difficult to get rid of it."

Aphrodite, "It was enough for you to get it drunk. That way, it would easily let go of you."

- "I wish I knew this. In a nutshell, it was not a good trip."

The guys smiled at her and politely said good-bye.

Brian, "Let's see, can you travel to other planets?"

Mitra, "Not us, only the animals and angels."

Brian, "Why not you?"

Eros, "That is how Izad wants it. We are human beings, one of the most vigorous creatures in Pardis. Izad had restricted us to do some things, including leaving Pardis."

Brian, "Now, tell me what is this Davaalpaa that she was talking about?"

"Guys, finally there is someone who asks more questions than me," said Anahita with a wild laugh.

Everyone laughed.

Brian, "Well, if *you* come to the Earth, you would ask the same amount of questions for sure."

Aphrodite laughed, "It is okay Brian. Ask us any questions you have. Davaalpaa is a stupid creature. His torso looks like a human, but it has twisted legs. Since it is always alone, as soon as it sees someone, it curls around him and will not let go. It is very persistent."

Brian, "I got it. Something like a tick. By the way, guys, I want to tell you something. I want to know whether I can look around Pardis and see all of it entirely? Maybe I will never come back here."

Eros, "No. You have to go back to your planet as soon as possible."

Mitra, "Don't spoil it, Eros. He can stay."

Eros, "You know what will happen if Izad knows about this? We will undergo the same ordeal of Adam and Eve, even worse."

Aphrodite, "I think it is okay as long as everything seems normal."

They laughed on the way to every subject, and when they got home, Brian felt happy and forgot his sad thoughts.

At home,

Eros, "Guys, we go straight to the dining hall. Brian, just explain what is necessary."

Brian, "Okay."

The door opened. One could hear the sound of music and laughter of the guests.

Brian, "Oh my god . . . who on earth are these guys?"

Mitra, "Heavenly beings . . . come with me . . ."

There were about thirty guests in the hall eating and drinking, including ten creatures that Brian had never seen before. He was staring at them with a feeling of awe.

Anahita softly said in Brian's ear, "Don't stare at them like that . . ."

Each of the guests was seated on a bed and the maids made sure they were comfortable.

Eros, "Let's introduce you to our friends one at a time."

The beds were scattered across the hall, with plenty of space in the middle of the hall where the fairies were dancing and cheering.

On the first bed, a young boy was sitting with a very pretty face. Brian looked at him. The boy was so charming as if a sculptor had sculpted him with extreme elegance.

Mitra, "Hi, Bethis. I want to meet you, my friend."

- "Hi, Brian."

- "I am glad to see you."

However, the next one was a girl with a few male servants around her, her hair was much longer than the rest of the women, so much that it was spread on the floor.

Aphrodite, "Brian, this lady is a close friend of mine."

- "Hello, I am Hera."

- "And I am Brian."

The boys and girls were introduced one by one and Brian was impatient to meet those special creatures.

On one of the beds, a girl and a boy had embraced each other and were caressing each other.

Brian, "Anahita, isn't it forbidden to have sex in someone else's house?"

- "It is, but these are husband and wife."

- "So, does that mean that a couple can do whatever they want wherever they want?"

- "Yes, of course."

Sitting on the next bed was a very beautiful creature about the size of a human being with a bird's body and the head of a very beautiful woman.

- "Hello, I am Alconost."

Brian had never heard such a pleasant voice. He wanted to sit and talk to her for hours.

Mitra, "Brian, I see you have already met my friend, Alconost?"

Brian forced a smile as he turned to Alconost, ((Yes. And I am so pleased to meet her.))

Brian took Mitra's hand and pulled her to a corner, "Tell me what the hell is Alconost?"

- "Alconost is a creature in our land."

- "Let's see. Do all of these creatures have the aptitude to speak and think and so on?"

- "Of course . . ."

- "I have to film all of this. I am sure Tom will go crazy by watching this. Well, we go ahead now and you introduce me to each one of them."

- "Okay. Follow me . . ."

The next one was a creature with a lion's body, eagle's head, and ears of a horse.

Brian was pointing the camera very subtly, "Tom, look at this. The joint production of a lion, an eagle, and a horse."

Mitra, "Brian, I am going to introduce you to Bashkoch."

Bashkoch, "Hi, Mitra's friend is our friend too."

Brian, "I am glad to see you, Bashkoch. Hope to see more of you a lot."

They passed by Bashkoch . . .

Brian, "Let's see. This gentleman, Bashkoch, was male, right? What is his job?"

Mitra, "He is the guardian of the Izads' treasures . . ."

However, the next creature was very similar to an owl.

Brian, "I know this one . . . This is Mr. Owl. We have birds like these on Earth."

"Why don't you take anything seriously?" asked Mitra angrily.

Brian pointed the camera toward Mitra, "Tom, I am going to introduce you to the most beautiful being in the universe, Mitra. The most beautiful and best girl I have ever met."

Mitra laughed, "Okay, now let me introduce you to the one that you call owl."

- "Well, isn't it an owl?"

Mitra, "No, it is Ashozushta. Izad created Ashozushta to confront Ahriman. It is very wise and has full knowledge of the holy book. It knows all the sciences."

Brian, "Are you serious? Well, maybe it can help us."

- "You should know that it is a friend of Izad, though . . ."

- "For now, let's go meet it . . . Hi, Ashozushta, I am Brian. Mitra talks a lot about you, I really wanted to talk to you too."

Ashozushta, "You remind me of an old friend."

Brian, "who?"

- "We ought not to talk about him at all. It is forbidden to talking about him."

Brian, "Adam? Or Eve?"

Ashozushta remained silent.

- "If he was a friend, then why didn't you help him?"

- "We helped him, Adam's son. I sent my children to exile because of him."

Mitra felt angst in her heart. Ashozushta turned to Mitra.

- "Fear not Mitra. Our guest will have no problems."

Brian, "I want to go back to Earth. can you help me?"

- "Paradise was not an attractive place for you?"

- "No, not at all . . . here everything is the same. No one strives for some purpose. Life is meaningless."

- "You are just like your father . . . Mitra, leave me alone with our guest."

Mitra nodded and walked away.

- "Well, Adam's son, what do you want from me?"

- "Show me the way back and repair my ship."

- "I can't show you the way back because in that case, you will learn how to come here. But I can teleport your body to the Earth in the blink of an eye. But you must promise me something."

- "What?"

- "You will not talk to anyone about what you saw."

Brian paused and continued, "Tell me how can the body be teleported from here to the Earth or from Earth to here in an instance?"

- "Your very being is knowledgeable . . . that is merit . . ."

- "But that was not the answer to my question . . ."

- "Well, there *are* portals, but not like what you may imagine. Going through these portals takes great courage . . ."

- "But you send me back to Earth, right?"

- "Of course . . . come see me tomorrow with Mitra . . ."

- "Meeting you gave me a feeling of hope. Thank you."

Brian breathed a sigh of relief. He went to the girls and discussed the matter with them.

Eros, "Thank Izad. So, others know about this too."

Anahita, "You deliberately invited Ashozushta to find out about Brian."

Brian ignored their conversation and asked Mitra, "Do you think I can trust it?"

Mitra, "Brian, this is not Earth. We only read about lies in the treasures of science. Here when someone says something, you can fully trust him."

- "You know what, Mitra? If we humans were like this, the Earth would be even more beautiful than the Paradise."

- "Well, what is the way you are over there?"

- "Most of the time we are not true to our word. We even hurt each other. We betray."

Mitra, "Perchance because you love power. Well, with all the wrong you do to each other, no wonder you feel lonely. Isn't it?"

- "Apparently not. Maybe we got used to all this bad stuff. Honestly, even our friendships are not real."

- "What about your loves? Are they real . . ."

Brian remained silent and dropped his head.

Mitra, "I wish it were real . . ."

Brian, "Look, Mitra. We, humans, are a collection of good and bad things. When you see one of us, you can't judge whether he or she is an absolute good or an absolute bad."

Eros, "Let's have some fun, guys."

He grabbed Mitra and Brian's hands and took them amidst the dancers and everyone danced and rejoiced.

Mitra danced but she was actually in another world, immersed in her dream, as a hand grabbed her hand. It was Brian who grasped her hand and led her to the hall's gate. When they reached the gate, he said, "Let's go to my room . . ."

There was a fire burning in Brian that tied his heart firmly to the love of Mitra. He closed the room's door and led Mitra to the bed as he kissed her.

Mitra, "I want you to know something about me . . ."

- "What?"

- "I don't know about other people, but when I say to someone that I like her, I really like her."

Brian lifted Mitra and lay her on the bed. He lay beside her and whispered softly in her ear,

- "I do not say I am in love. Because when I leave, I can at least fool myself that the pain I have to suffer on Earth is not the pain of love, it is a pain of liking someone and passes by."

Then he kissed Mitra's lips slowly, Mitra had closed her eyes.

- "You know what?"

- "What?"

- "The pain of love accelerates aging . . ."

A tear drops ran down from the corner of Brian's eye. He raised his head and kissed Mitra from head to toe. He embraced her.

Mitra, "Something has engulfed my whole being . . ."

- "This is the heat of intercourse that goes along being loved."

Brian said as he immersed himself in Mitra, "My pretty one ... my most beautiful one, I wish you were the only thing I could take with me to the Earth."

The lovemaking between them lasted for hours, and they were so lost in each other's love that they even forgot about themselves.

The dawn was at hand and the light was brighter.

Brian, "Can I sleep in your arms?"

- "Sleep."

- "When I fall asleep you can go if you like."

- "I don't like it. I want to stay with you as long as you are here."

Brian closed his eyes and fell asleep . . .

Brian was sitting in his office. He was shuffling the papers and documents as he heard the sound of the door opening and the light hit Brian's eyes hard. A little girl came in with golden hair and honey eye color. She was wearing a short floral dress and had a beautiful flower tiara on her hair, holding a small teddy bear. She looked four or five years old.

- "Hi, Dad . . ."

- "Hellooo, daddy's cute girl . . . Wow, how beautiful you look with your flower tiara. Give me the energizing kiss."

The little girl kissed Brian.

- "Daaad . . ."

- "What, daddy sweetie . . ."

- "Mom won't let us go to Ella's birthday . . ."

- "Oh no . . . daddy's girls quarrel again."

Mitra entered the room. She was wearing a deep blue top and jeans. Her hair was shorter. Her face, however, was beautiful and radiant without makeup. There were quite a few handbags in her right hand and a tray with two cups of coffee in her left hand. Brian was kneeling to talk to the little girl and got up as he saw Mitra.

Mitra, "I brought you coffee."

- "Why did you bother. You could have said you were coming, and I would tell the secretary to make coffee for us."

He took the tray from Mitra.

- "The coffee I make is something else, you said that . . ."

- "Why can't I see enough of you, Mitra. When will be the day that I wake up in the morning to see you have become an ordinary person to me."

Mitra sat on the coach and put the sacks beside her.

- "Never. Never. Never. I would kill you if someday you tell me I have become an ordinary person."

- "Daaad, you were going to fix my delinquent."

Mitra, "Yes, that's right. You are supposed to resolve the dispute between us."

- "Why am I not allowed to go to my friend's birthday?"

- "Because I have a lot of ins and outs."

Brian, "Well, tell me your reasons . . ."

Mitra, "Today, Ms. Lara broke Mr. George's glass with a ball, shaved Ms. Daisy dog's hair with your new shaver."

Brian laughed loudly, and Mitra gazed at him. Brian swallowed his laughter.

- "Well, Ms. Lara, we conclude that your mother is right . . . Why did you do that?"

- "I didn't break the glass, dad. I just kicked the ball and it was the ball that broke the glass of Mr. George's house. And about Ms. Daisy, I wanted to help. Ms. Daisy herself said she was going to cut her dog's hair because of the heat. So, when she told mom to watch her dog for a few hours until she came back, I helped her out to cut the trouble short."

Mitra pressed her teeth together with great rage.

- "Oh, Brian, you don't know how embarrassed I was. She had shaved a crossroads right in the middle of the poor dog's scalp. Ms. Daisy almost had a stroke when she saw it. Moreover, in order to motivate your mom to lose weight, she has cut down all clothes in her wardrobe to reduce their size."

Brian's eyes widened in surprise, "So, Lara, what did your grandmother do when she saw that scene?"

Lara, "She said it doesn't matter. She was going to throw all those clothes away and instead, get some new ones."

Mitra, "She said that for she didn't want you to be punished."

Lara, "Well, then don't punish me."

- "No way. You have been very cheeky lately."

Brian, now that Lara stated caused acceptable to the court, and on the other hand, you are right as well, how about changing the kind of punishment. For example, instead of not going to her friend's birthday, spends the weekend with her grandmother and we go on a trip for two? Huh?"

Lara, "But, daaaddy . . ."

Brian, "You decide, Lara. Birthday or weekend?"

Mitra, "Yeah, it's a good idea."

Lara, "I choose my birthday. Because are all my friends are there. I prefer hanging out with my friends to you two who always think about punishing me."

Mitra and Brian smiled at each other. Mitra got up and went to Brian, who was leaning against his desk.

- "Well, then you've solved another problem of ours."

Brian kissed Mitra's lips and woke up. He was still in Mitra's arms. He looked at Mitra. She had closed her eyes too.

- "Mitra, come with me to the Earth . . . You can come back here via those portals whenever you want."

- "You stay for my sake . . ."

- "I can't . . ."

- "I can't either because a person who can use those portals must have a record of being present at least once in both places of origin and destination, and one may go through these portals only by the order of Izad."

Brian was immersed in thought.

- "Don't you have any information about Adam and Eve after their deportation to Earth? That is, can't you check in the memoir's room what happened to Adam and Eve had on Earth?"

Mitra, "No. Not in the memoir's room. The memoir's room is only about what happened in Pardis, but maybe we can find something about them in my dad's *secrets of the forgotten room*. Of course, if my dad had brought that part of the secrets with him here."

- "How?"

- "Well, some time ago, he brought some of his belongings here so that he could spend more time with us. As far as I know, he only brought part of the secret's room here."

- "So how can we find out?"

- "Just go to his room and look for the memoir."

- "So, what are you waiting for? Let's go . . ."

Brian and Mitra entered a circular hall with very tall walls and ceiling, so large that the ceiling could not be seen. The room had an area of about 11,000 square feet. The walls were made of live wood. They were alive because they had moving foliage, and all walls had windows that were covered with a transparent goo. Each window had a different view. Mitra took Brian's hand and led him to the center of the circle which had a surface of marble, with beautiful motifs in the center.

"From the moment of transgression, Adam . . ." said Mitra loudly.

The surface began to rotate and move upwards. They passed by different windows, and Brian saw a different landscape through each window.

Brian, "What's going on with these windows?"

- "Each of the windows is about a particular creature who has either become mortal or has committed a sin and been deported or has left Pardis for an important matter. Only the servants of the Izad's court are allowed to enter this room."

- "Well, you are not one of the court servants. Are you?"

- "Nope."

- "Well, what if someone finds out we have come here?"

- "Then my father is responsible for our punishment."

Brian stared at Mitra.

Mitra, "What's wrong?"

- "Nothing. I think I have ruined your life since I came here."

- "I am fine. I am all okay. Don't worry."

The surface of the circle rotated to a higher height and stopped next to a window.

Mitra, "Here it is."

- "What should we do now? How does it open?"

- "Just push away the goo from the top of it."

Brian pulled off the substance by his hand. It was very sticky and hard to remove, and this was the first time that he had difficulty to do a task in Pardis. It took a while and with Mitra's help, he was able to push it away, and after removing all of it, a tremendous force sucked them in. They appeared on a glass surface. Brian was scared and for a moment he felt that he was suspended in the air. He looked under his feet. It was as if he was looking down at the ground from the sky. A tired, helpless man was walking on the ground in the desert. He was anxious.

Mitra, "Brian, this dude is your father."

- "Yes, I see. I saw him in the memoirs' room, but not so wasted."

Brian watched the passage of day and night and the wandering of Adam. After a few days, Adam reached a jungle, exhausted and tired. While he was starved of hunger and thirst, he shouted and called Izad. He fell to the ground and passed out. Eve was standing beside a tree, caressing a bird, while she had no clothes like Adam and her only cover was her long hair. When she heard Adam's voice, she ran toward him and saw Adam has fallen to the ground. She got closer and hugged him. She kissed Adam and rested his head on her legs.

Adam slowly opened his eyes and said, "We are mortal now. We will perish, Eve . . ."

- "Fear not, Adam. Someone is here to help us."

Adam put his hand on the ground and got up with difficulty, "Who? Izad has come to see us?"

"No, Gabriel has come," Eve sighed.

Gabriel slowly came out from behind the trees, sat beside Adam and stroked his face, "Hi my friend, why are you so upset?"

- "I will perish."

- "You will not perish . . . I am here to help you."

Eve, "I was just like you. I didn't know what to do until Gabriel came and said we needed to eat and drink because we were mortals."

Gabriel, "Earth's climate is different from Pardis. Besides, you have a new body and you have to be able to reconcile these two."

Adam, "Where is Izad? Did it send you? I need to talk to it. Please help, Gabriel."

- "Forgive me, my friend, but I am not allowed to talk about Izad with you. You will not be allowed to see its face anymore. I will be with you for a while, for a short time. So you learn how to live on Earth. There are a few things I have to teach you (he handed over a necklace to Eve) and then if you need to summon me you should blow on this necklace. Then I will appear to you."

Eve put the necklace around her neck.

Days passed and Gabriel taught them how to live on the land and how to hunt, eat and drink. it provided them with clothing from the leaves of the trees to protect them from heat and cold and chose a small, dark cave as their home for their comfort and safety. Since Adam was a skilled warrior, he defended himself and Eve very well against the beasts, but life was hard. There was a huge difference between that ageless and beautiful Paradise and this terrifying and unknown Earth.

Every time Adam and Eve wept, the sky became cloudy.

Brian, "Why does the sky get cloudy every time they cry?"

Mitra, "The sky is cloudy only when Izads is sad, at least that is the case in Pardis."

They both looked at the image below their feet, and Brian suddenly saw someone in the darkness of the woods. His face was not visible.

Brian said loudly, "Mitra, what is it?"

- "What?"

- "Right there . . . it is hiding behind a tree."

Mitra felt sad at the bottom of her heart and sighed unknowingly.

Brian stared at Mitra, "What is the matter?"

- "It is Izad . . . gone to peep at Adam and Eve."

- "Why secretly?"

- "So none question its justice."

Brian was silent. Another scene appeared below their feet. Adam and Eve were having sex with each other, but Adam pushed Eve away, "Sorry Eve, but I can't."

Eve, "Why? Do you hate me? It was my fault that this you happened to."

- "No Eve. Not at all . . . I still love you, but I can't take so much pain. My body feels the pain, so does my soul. I can't, Eve. I want to die. Let's kill ourselves and get rid of so much pain. Better not to exist at all."

Tears ran down Eve's cheeks and she held Adam's hands, "It is better to end this life with you than to endure it."

They got up and went out of the cave, but Gabriel suddenly appeared in front of them, "What is the matter, my friend? You have become frustrated so soon . . . I have a message for you. You know if you drop this test unfinished you will not be released again but you will be doomed to hell. There is eternal life, and of course very painful . . . so listen to the new orders of Izad.

"His majesty, the creator and ruler of beings, ordered that from this moment on, you will live a quieter life and have children. Izad has granted you the sleep phenomenon to soothe your tired soul and body in the darkness of the night and If you successfully pass Izad's test on Earth, you will go to the second Pardis after fulfilling your life on Earth. As of now, life will be easier for you."

Adam knelt and cried. He looked up at the sky and shouted, "So you didn't forget us. Forgive me . . . forgive us."

Eve sat down beside Adam and they both cried.

Eve, "Even if you don't like to talk to us, we know now that you can hear us. At least we can talk to you even if you don't want to answer us. Forgive me and that's enough for me. I don't want eternal life if you let me know you have forgiven us. All my life, I will be in debt from you and Adam."

Adam took Eve's hand and calmed her down. Gabriel led them to the cave and provided them with a bed in the cave and asked them to lie down together. Eve lay next to Adam and rested her head on Adam's shoulder. They closed their eyes and fell asleep.

Brian sat down and said sadly, "Poor guys . . . Izad's arrogance caused Adam and Eve to fall like this."

Mitra, "Don't say that, Izad is not arrogant at all."

- "You don't have to defend it. As much as it is your god, it is my god as well."

- "But you don't know it."

- "Don't talk to me about knowing. For each of us, god is measured by the hardship or comfort that it was intended for us. How can you understand me when you and your family have lived your lives in abundance and plenty? You have neither felt the cold nor the heat . . . neither tasted pain nor felt hunger . . . Yes, in your opinion, Izad should be compassionate, but in my view, as half of my people live in abject poverty and they are oppressed every day, Izad is a selfish, arrogant being . . . "

Mitra stared at Brian in silence and astonishment.

A few moments later, Brian calmed down a bit and came round, "I am sorry. I was upset a little bit and went too far. I am sorry to be so harshly to you."

Mitra, who saw a different man in front of her, was not upset at all and unlike what Brian thought, his boldness that she had never experienced in Pardis had fascinated Mitra even more.

Brian, "What? Why are you looking at me like that?"

- "You are different . . . a lot . . ."

Brian sighed coldly, "Thanks for reminding me every so often."

Mitra and Brian went back to the window.

"We leave the room," said Mitra quietly.

As they went out, the room's surface spiraled down like a circular elevator. Brian was staring at the windows. Mitra was also staring at Brian, who suddenly shouted, "Wait . . . look at that."

The surface stopped moving.

Mitra, "Where?"

- "In that window. Aren't they Angra Mainyu and Hormuzd?"

- "That's right. I want to see that memoir."

The couple entered through the window. But this time, they were not watching that memoir from above, they were in the scene. Hormuzd was standing by a gate. The scene was dark. Mitra and Brian went near him, but seemingly they were invisible since no one noticed them.

Brian, "Are we visible now?"

Mitra laughed, "You don't get used to anything, Brian. Of course not, this is just a memory of the past."

The gates were large and it seemed they were made of molten iron. Two guards with white clothing opened the gates and saluted Hormuzd. It was dark and dirty everywhere and there was the sound of screams. Wherever Hormuzd walked, flowers grew.

Brian, "Where is this? What are those sounds for?"

Mitra, "Here is a part of hell where Angra Mainyu and Iblis went into exile. Those sounds are the sounds of torture of those who have been banished to different levels of hell."

- "Did Izad order their torture?"

Mitra got angry, "I don't know why you are so pessimistic about Izad? How do you think it can torture someone? Their evil deeds are torturing them to cleanse their souls and when this period is over, they can go to Paradise II."

- "Does that mean even Iblis?"

- "Of course . . . if it admits its mistake and accepts it and then accepts the torture of its soul. But so far, it has not accepted it and I don't think it will ever do so . . . Its sin is so awful that has made Izad its enemy."

- "You are right."

As they walked behind Hormuzd, they looked at the dark, filthy scenes of Inferno. Mitra was more scared than Brian since she had never imagined such a place.

Hormuzd reached a house that looked like an old, abandoned factory. He went in. Some of the jinns had gathered in various groups at every corner like homeless people. There was no joy and comfort. The kids were imploring as they followed their mothers, and the women pushed away from their children as they were looking for a piece of bread. The men, as if coming back from the war, had each been leaning at a corner. When Hormuzd arrived, they all vacated the pathway to show respect. Women and children rubbed their faces to Hormuzd's footprints that had grown plants. Hormuzd entered a large tent without noticing them. Mitra and Brian followed him. Angra Mainyu was leaning on a bed and was sweating heavily and two persons were fanning him.

Upon seeing Hormuzd, Angra Mainyu said with a scornful tone, "See who has come to see us? My competent brother, the great commander of Izad's army, Lord Hormuzd. Tell me what brought you here?"

Hormuzd opened a board that was floating in the air and sat on it, "How are you, Angra Mainyu?"

- "Did you come here to ask how I am? As you see . . . I reign in Hell."

Hormuzd smiled, "Kingship? I thought Iblis must be the king of Hell . . . Well, you serve him anyway."

- "Of course . . . Of course . . . but Iblis is not here now. You know, Iblis and I, unlike all the creatures here, are not you and your lord's prisoners. Right, we are restricted, but we are living here. Iblis spends most of its time on Earth, and thus, I am the only king here."

- "We are aware of everything, Angra Mainyu. For example, the other day you and (he looked at the jinn around him that were skinny and impoverished) your so-called soldiers came up to the gates of the paradise of blessings. I don't know how do you think you can disobey Izad and be successful. You are still stupid, Angra Mainyu . . . clueless and selfish. I came here to tell you that you'd better avoid more punishment because Izad would not have mercy on you if it notices your clandestine operations. I will not tell Izad this time either, but if you repeat that once again I will make you regret your existence."

Angra Mainyu crushed the cup he had in his hand.

Hormuzd, "I wish I could help but, alas, it is not possible."

He said this and left. Angra Mainyu threw the cup behind Hormuzd with great anger and began sexually abusing two soldiers who had caused the failure of his operations in full view of others.

Bryan turned Mitra's face away to prevent her from seeing that horrible scene and they quickly went through the window and out of the secret's room.

Brian shouted as they got out, "Angra Mainyu is really disgusting."

"My room... .," exclaimed Mitra as she reached the door.

The door opened to a beautiful plain full of strange flowers and plants with a large bed in the middle. The plain's sky was a scene of the galaxy in yellow, green, purple and blue colors. The planets were suspended in the sky of Mitra's room like pretty round balls. There was a corridor at a corner of the plain, covered with bizarre moving plants as if it was a passageway that connected the plain to another place. At the other corner, various strange musical instruments were moving and practicing, but no sound was heard.

"Is this your room?" asked Brian while fascinatedly looking around, "Did you decorate it yourself? It is really wonderful."

- "Thank you. Yes, I made it myself. The rooms are built according to our imagination."

- "What beautiful imagination you have. What is that corridor for?"

- "That? Follow me if you like to see it . . ."

Brian and Mitra crossed the corridor and entered a large cavern. Upon arrival, it seemed they were suspended in the air and amongst the stars.

Mitra, "It has been a while that I have been investigating different galaxies and this is part of my research."

- "Oh my God. This is the most beautiful thing I have ever seen in my life. It is great, like you."

He rubbed his face and gazed into her eyes, "Wow, Mitra, I had never seen you blinking at this close distance. You have an extra membrane in your eye that covers your eyes every once in a while. It is scary . . . Are all of you like this?"

Mitra laughed, "Of course, Brian . . . This is normal. We have two eyelids."

- "But we are not like that."

- "I know . . . However, we do not belong to the human race and there are differences between us."

- "That is right. We are like trees that have taken root at two different places."

He said this and kissed Mitra's lips.

All of a sudden, one of Mitra's maids appeared. Brian cried out in fear.

- "Oh, my god. Didn't they teach you to ask for permission before making an appearance?"

Mitra, "Brian, the maids do not ask for permission here."

- "That means they come in whenever they want."

- "Yes."

- "Does that mean they come even if you are in the middle of some monkey business?"

Mitra smiled at Brian and addressed the maidservant, "What's up?"

- "Ma'am, there is an invitation for you."

- "From who?"

The maid waved her hand in the air and a full-size image of Hormuzd appeared. At the same time, the sisters quickly entered Mitra's room and upon seeing Hormuzd's apparition, quietly stood beside the door.

Hormuzd began to speak, "My children, I have thrown a party today, to which you are all invited. I will meet you at the party to spend some happy time together."

After the speech, the Hormuzd hologram disappeared. The maid bowed and left the room.

Eros, "What should we do now?"

Mitra, "About what?"

Eros replied angrily, "Do you dig the depth of the disaster? We granted refuge to an alien in our land. We broke the law. We should immediately go to Ashozushta to send him back home. On the other hand, the Hormuzd's party. . . If we don't go there . . ."

Aphrodite, "We must go . . ."

Brian, "Well, we can go see Ashozushta after the party."

Aphrodite, "So, you stay home until we come back . . ."

Brian, "What the . . . ! Are you kidding me? This is the best opportunity for me to meet you all at once."

Eros, "No way, Brian. Please don't make more trouble."

Anahita, "We can take him with us by changing his appearance . . ."

Mitra, "Yeah, changing his appearance is a great idea . . . Aphrodite, you can do it."

Eros, "No . . . Aphrodite, you won't."

Anahita, "Stop it, Eros. There will be no problem. We can turn him into a Twister."

Aphrodite, "I agree with Eros."

Mitra, "But, Aphrodite, it is better for us too."

Suddenly, Brian raised his hand and said loudly, "Stop it . . . You are talking non-stop . . . Wait, I will tell you what to do. First, Anahita, tell me about the transformation?"

Anahita, "We can turn you into a small creature for a little while and take you with us to the party. However, among us, only Aphrodite has the science of transformation."

Brian, "Well, Eros. What is the problem with this?"

Eros, "Look, Brian, all the authorities of the land are there and we can't get away if you create a problem or get into trouble."

Anahita, "As I said, we turn it into a Twister, and when it wraps around my wrist, there will be no suspicion."

Brian, "Wait, what the hell is the Twister?"

Mitra, "A crawling plant used to decorate the body."

- "Well, what if there is a problem and I remain a Twister forever?"

Anahita, "There will be no problem, Brian. Under any circumstances, you will return to your original form after a short time. Moreover, Aphrodite is very skilled in this job, so you don't have to worry."

Brian, "Great. So, I become a Twister and go to the party and get to know your relatives. It just changes my appearance, but my mind stays the same, right? I mean, can I perceive the environment?"

The girls laughed.

Aphrodite, "Affirmative, Brian. Don't worry, you are yourself, just in another body."

- "Okay, when will I change shape?"

Aphrodite, "We go to my room right now and we are done."

The guys led Brian to Aphrodite's room. Aphrodite's room was like a forest where many unearthly animals lived. Upon arriving, Aphrodite quickly went toward a strange animal about seven feet high that was covered in scales but had the body of a camel. Brian was frightened by its awful appearance and backed away, "What is *that thing*, Aphrodite?"

- "It is a Donal . . . In Pardis, animals do not harm anyone. You can get close to it."

- "Oh, it is so strange. I have never seen an animal like this."

Suddenly a beautiful bird with feathers the color of various hues of purple flew inside and landed on Aphrodite's shoulder. The bird's feathers were glowing and subcutaneously scattered light rays showed through its body.

Brian, "Wow, these are wonderful."

Aphrodite, "All are mine, both plants and animals . . . I raised them myself."

Mitra, "Brian, there is not much time."

Brian, "Oh. . . yes, you are right. . . we have to get on with it. Well, I'm ready."

Aphrodite pointed to a bed and said, "Okay Brian, please take off your clothes and lie on this bed."

Brian, "What? My clothes? All of them?"

Aphrodite, "Well, of course . . ."

- "But, I . . . I . . . am not comfortable in front of you."

Anahita, "Well, we will get naked too if you like, so you will not feel bad about it."

- "No thanks. I think it would be better if only I get naked."

Brian felt very uncomfortable. He took off his clothes. The girls stared at his body.

Eros, "Oh, my God. He is a bit different . . ."

Aphrodite, "It is due to Earth's environment. Look at his willy . . ."

Brian, "Guys, please don't comment on my body and do your job sooner."

Aphrodite went over Brian's head and uttered some sentences in an unknown language. Brian felt dizzy and passed out. When he opened his eyes, everything was much larger than normal. He checked himself. He looked like wet branches of a tree. He felt the moisture on his body.

Mitra, "Are you okay, Brian?"

- "I don't know . . . Well, this is the first time I have become a piece of wood. I think I am very, very small, but these blossoms are pretty."

Aphrodite lifted Brian and put him on Anahita's wrist, "Well, Brian, wrap your body around Anahita's wrist and stick to her hand."

Brian, "Anahita, can I see myself in the mirror?"

- "Of course."

Anahita went to the door and said, "Hall of mirrors . . ."

She entered the hall of mirrors and held her hand against the mirror.

"Damn it... .," Brian shouted, "What the heck is that? I have really become a blossoming branch. Are these two blossoms my eyes?"

- "Of course, Brian, but you'd better be cool. I remember the first time I became a little dancer, I was excited like this too. Okay, Brian. You can detach yourself from my hand so I can get ready."

- "Sure, I close my eyes so you feel more comfortable."

Anahita smiled and said, "Thanks."

The girls were ready and lined up in the main hall and after reviewing their to-do list, started out.

They passed through a forest of colorful trees and reached the green lakes. A guard was standing by the lake. He bowed as he saw the girls, and Eros handed him the invitation card. The guard opened an invisible gate and a bridge appeared on the lake. The bridge was made of glass and its handles were halos of light. The width of the bridge was about 50 feet and its length, which was equal to the length of the lake, was hundreds of miles. They proceeded to walk on the bridge. A little ahead of them, two handsome men were walking hand in hand.

Brian, "Who are those two? Are they your relatives?"

Mitra, "No, the Audits are all heterosexual, they are another strain of human being."

Brian shouted, "What? You mean they are gay? And here in Paradise, for that matter?"

The girls stopped.

Mitra, "Brian, please control yourself. If you make noises like this, you will blow everything as soon as we arrive."

- "Pardon me, I just got a little excited. (He lowered his voice) now tell me what is between these two?"

Eros, "They are a couple . . . partners . . . bedmates . . ."

- "I can't believe this . . ."

Eros, "What is the problem?"

- "Well, two men got married, that is, they have intercourse. On Earth, it is a great sin for two homosexuals to have sex, forbidden . . . We are told that if we do this, we will never go to Heaven, and now it is commonplace here in the heart of Paradise."

Aphrodite said angrily, "Forbidden? Maybe these guys don't know much about the Earth, but I know there is a lot of cruelty and corruption. Tell me how do you consider something that doesn't hurt anyone a sin? It totally depends on personal taste and I think suppressing a feeling that doesn't hurt anyone is a greater sin."

Brian was silent.

Anahita, "Does that mean you have to marry a member of the opposite sex even if you don't have any feeling for that person just because it is a sin?"

- "That is right . . . However, in some countries, they handle this situation better in recent years."

Eros, "As such, you do great wrong to both yourself and the member of the opposite sex you are married to. I think it is a bigger sin."

"I am not gay, Eros, and I don't like to talk about it," said Brian, whose opinion on this matter was slightly different.

They went across the lake and another guard opened another invisible gate, and the bridge extended across the sky above the colorful trees. They passed over the trees and reached a large marble building that was suspended in the air. Water fountains were soaring around the palace but disappeared before they could descend. They set foot on the marble palace's courtyard from the bridge. The fairies greeted them.

Brian, "Is this Hormuzd's estate?"

Aphrodite, "This is one of the Hormuzd's mansions . . . Izad has given him many palaces in all areas of Pardis . . ."

Brian looked around, the statues in various spots of the palace were made of a strange material. It was as if the three-dimensional sculptures were made of blue, purple and green lights.

The weather was more pleasant there, and Brian wondered what supported the suspended palace in the air while there was nothing other than the floating building. The girls climbed white stairs and reached a large hall. Short, beautiful fairies with naked female bodies and golden wings were dancing at a height of seven feet above the surface and the sound of laughter was heard from every corner of the hall.

Eros, "We'd better break up and each goes to a different corner. Anahita, remember not to mingle too much with others."

They separated from each other. Anahita began to walk toward a random direction but suddenly stopped and greeted an imaginary being that Brian could not see. As she passed by the being, Brian asked, "What was that? Why didn't I see it?"

- "What was that you didn't see?"

- "You were talking to something, what was it and why didn't I see it?"

- "It was a strain of the jinn and you couldn't see it because your eyes are mortal . . . or maybe because you don't use all of your brains."

- "Excuse me?"

- "Well, I work on the body anatomy of many creatures and I know that every part of the brain does something and if you don't use it, you will lose it. Probably, that is your problem."

A girl was approaching Anahita. She was young and pretty. Anahita happily hugged her and said, "Hi, mom. I had to come to you first. Please forgive me, I was lost in the clutter."

Mehraveh smiled and said, "No problem, my pretty one . . ."

The only thing that made anyone look older than the others was the amount of respect shown by those around that person. The sound of laughter and music filled the air. There was no sign of hypocrisy and flattery or showing off at the party. They were all happy and enjoying themselves together. No one meddled in other people's business until a bell rang. They all lined up in regular rows and stood facing a platform placed above the staircase. Hormuzd and Sepandarmaz arrived and greeted everyone. The guests bowed in response.

Hormuzd, "Good evening, my children . . . I am glad to see you here on this delightful day. I have not been in Pardis for a while and missed the opportunity to take care of you. This is a party for us to increase our happiness and joy. Enjoy."

They all dispersed and went to their own corners of the hall, and some encircled Hormuzd.

Brian thought to himself, 'Look, he has brought his children and taken over the whole Paradise, while our father ate an apple and we were displaced like this."

Suddenly, Anahita whispered, "That is not the case, Brian . . . You saw how hard Hormuzd worked for Pardis."

A little further on, Aphrodite urged Anahita to be quiet.

Brian, "Let's see, how did you read my mind?"

- "Be quiet . . . Here, everyone can read your mind if they concentrate on it."

Brian, "Thanks for telling me."

Brian noticed wonderful scenes of love and longing between them. Since Anahita was very playful and naughty, she was not too much involved with the crowd. Brian was immersed in the surroundings as he spotted Mitra from afar at a corner of the garden petting and kissing in the arms of a young man.

Brian, "Anahita, that must be Mitra or am I wrong?"

- "Yes, that is Mitra . . . What's the matter?"

- "Who is the man?"

- "Tirdad, a cousin . . . he has already been sleeping with Mitra for a couple of times."

- "My God . . . I can't believe it . . . When will we leave here?"

- "Leave? The party has just begun . . . where to go?"

- "I don't know, take me out of here . . . anywhere except here . . ."

- "Okay, let's go, but if the guards are at the gate, they will be suspicious of me leaving here, we have to sneak out . . ."

They went to the door which was suspended in the air.

Anahita said quietly, "Garden of Mitra's house . . ."

She opened the door and entered Mitra's mansion.

Anahita, "Tell me what happened, Brian?"

- "Nothing . . . I want to be myself again . . ."

- "Okay, wait, we go to Aphrodite's room and I will do it for you."

Anahita converted Brian back to normal, then they boarded a chariot and went to a mountain. The chariot ascended to the height of the peak, then both got off and sat at the summit.

At the party, Mitra was looking for Anahita. Tirdad approached her from behind and hugged her, "Mitra, we can spend the night together if you feel like it."

- "No, Tirdad, tonight I will be with someone else."

Mitra had a strange feeling. In Pardis, one could spend each night with a different person. There was no sign of attachment or passion, but Mitra had fallen for Brian.

Tiradad kissed Mitra and said, "Okay. . . until the day I am in eternal Paradise, it could be a night to be together."

- "I don't think I can . . ."

At the mountain peak, Bryan and Anahita were staring at their surroundings.

Brian, "This place makes you forget your anger . . . very quiet. . . I mean this Pardis . . ."

- "Well, yeah . . . here the resources are sustainable . . . They do not perish and are not created. You may have all of this on the Earth, but because they are your own handiwork, there have some disadvantages."

Brian smiled and said, "You don't look so much knowledgeable. . ."

- "Yeah, because I am so naughty . . . Did you feel bad to see Mitra with Tirdad? Did you spend the last night with her?"

- "Well, you know . . . I have spent many nights with women and in the morning put them aside . . . But, I mean I put them aside, do you know what I am saying? I don't know, maybe what I did with them was similar to what Mitra does, but I did not show any interest in them."

- "Brian, nothing around here is like Earth. We do not attach to anyone and we love everyone but we do not adhere to anyone . . . It doesn't matter to us with whom we spend the night until we get married."

- "This is very painful . . . We have a name for people like you, *prostitute*, and they are considered low-class in our community. . . They frown on these women or sometimes even on the Johns."

- "Why, do they violate someone's rights? Or do those who make love to them, do it by force?"

- "No . . ."

- "Well, if someone doesn't like it, he can avoid that person . . . I believe you have ridiculous laws on the Earth . . .

However, about Mitra . . . I noticed that she has changed after meeting you."

- "When I saw him with that jerk of a boy, I remembered our last night's conversation. For a moment, I thought she was treating me like a marionette. She is toying with me whenever she wants."

- "I don't know what a marionette is? But I know you have fallen for the wrong girl. Brian, you two will not understand each other and none are to blame, so you'd better not think of her . . . You don't know the meaning of our behaviors, and we don't know that of yours either . . . Enjoy your stay here."

Brian threw his arm around Anahita's shoulders and said, "Yeah, my dear friend . . . I think you're right . . . Everything is fine now, but I wish we had some cigarettes."

- "Cigarette? What is that?"

- "A cool thing . . . Something made of tobacco, paper, and a filter. You light it up and inhale its smoke into your lungs. It is fatal to consume a lot of it, but it feels good at the moment . . . However, I think that is no problem for you since you are immortal, but I love it . . ."

- "So, it seems you are really in a bad condition that you prefer to die sooner but feel fine for a moment."

- "Well, not as much as you think, but yeah . . . I think something like that . . ."

- "It is awful to hurt your body . . . you don't take care of it and surely Izad will be angry with you . . . I have to investigate tobacco."

- "Come on, Anahita. It is better to enjoy the scenery."

Brian pointed to the distance. The nice colored sky and Pardis were below them in all their glory.

Brian, "I had never seen such splendor before . . . It is so much like the Earth, but more magnificent . . ."

- "Well, I have not noticed that before, but I think you are right, it is very nice."

- "Tell me how do you build these houses? They are so peculiar . . . without any walls, every room has a separate natural space. That is great."

- "These are constructed by Izad in a natural way."

- "Whatever they are, they look wonderful."

They both stared ahead in silence.

The three sisters were looking for Anahita at the party and since they could not find her, they gathered at a corner.

Eros, "One of us must connect to her mind and see where she is."

Mitra, "I will do it . . ."

Mitra closed her eyes and searched for Anahita.

Anahita, "Brian, Mitra is looking for us to find our place. Where should I tell her are we?"

- "How is she going to find it out?"

- "By telepathy."

- "Can you stop her?"

- "Yeah."

- "So, it would be better she doesn't know where we are. We will meet her when we return home . . . Well, Anahita, tell me a little about the behaviors of the human beings here . . ."

Brian and Anahita began a sweet conversation oblivious to all that happened in the past.

Mitra, "Anahita doesn't let me connect to her mind. perhaps they are out of the party."

Eros, "Well, the important thing is that they are not at the party and thus, there is no problem. They will return home wherever they are."

It was evening when Brian and Anahita entered the courtyard of Mitra's house, laughing boisterously.

An anxious Mitra was awaiting them at the mansion lawn, and upon seeing them, walked toward them and yelled, "Where the hell have you been?"

Anahita, who had never seen such an expression in any creature, wondered, "What is wrong with you, Mitra?"

- "Answer me. Where have you been until now? Where did you go together?"

Brian passed by her without answering and said to Anahita, "I go to my room, see you later."

Mitra followed him. They both went through the doorway and entered Brian's room.

Mitra pulled Brian's hands from behind and asked angrily, "What are you doing? Why is your behavior like this?"

Brian tried to keep his cool and asked calmly, "Which behavior?"

- "What are you doing? Where have you been and what were you doing with Anahita?"

It was as if Brian was waiting to hear that phrase from Mitra's mouth to lose his temper, "It is not your business, why you ask? huh? It is not your business. Did I ask you what were you doing in the arms of that scumbag? While you were with me the other night and you told me you loved me. Where I came from, even hookers aren't interested in people whom they are going to forget the next morning."

Tears ran down Mitra's cheeks and she said quietly, "I feel I am a mortal. I feel my soul is going to perish . . . I feel the thirst of wanting you . . . I don't know what is a hooker but I told Tirdad that I couldn't be with him. I don't know why I said that, but I know I'd love to be with you all the time."

Mitra could not speak, her throat was choked and tears had driven her mad. She decided to leave the room, but Brian stopped her. He slowly hugged her and kissed her lips while taking her to his bed in silence and angrily ripping off Mitra's clothes. Teardrops fell from Mitra's beautiful eyes. She surrendered himself to Brian. Brian stared at Mitra's face and said, "Don't look at any man while I am here . . . I can't stand it."

Mitra smiled and closed her eyes. Truly, she was a unique goddess. A couple of romantic minutes passed between them, but none of them wanted to leave the bed or the other person.

Mitra, "I wish I could sleep too . . . like Adam and Eve, maybe I would have suffered less pain."

- "I wish I could sleep and when I wake up, see that there is a hotel room and no matter who you are, I take your hand and take you home with me and will not let you go away."

Brian's eyelids felt heavy and he fell asleep while holding Mitra in his arms.

After a few hours of sleep, he opened his eyes and glanced at Mitra, "No, once again, it was not a dream and I am still here."

Mitra raised her head from Brian's shoulder, "Are you awake?"

- "Yep . . . waking up next to you is happiness itself . . . Mitra, I can't leave you for a minute, the feeling I have toward you is like a thirst for water, as the need for air. I want to spend every moment making love to you."

And he began kissing Mitra.

The housemaid appeared and Brian shouted. Mitra laughed out loud.

Maid, "Ma'am, your father is here."

Brian said to Mitra angrily, "As long as I am here, instruct them to ask for permission and then enter."

- "Okay, Brian, (facing the maid) Where are the sisters?"

- "They are with your father in the reception hall, and your mother will also be there in a moment."

- "Brian, don't you come down . . ."

- "But why? Look, Mitra, we have to find the portals . . . so, there will no longer be any boundaries between us."

- "Only a few people know about the portals, even my father knows nothing about them."

- "How do you know that? Maybe we can find something in the Memoirs Room or your father's Secrets Room."

- "Why don't we ask Ashozushta to do it?"

- "Because I am sure he won't let you come to Earth with me, he will never reveal the secrets of those portals to me and will send me straight to Earth without allowing me to figure it out."

Mitra thought for a moment and said, "If Ashozushta is not going to help us, I believe there is someone else who might help."

- "Who?"

- "Well, the only person who openly uses those portals is Hormuzd and in Pardis, only one person might understand us."

"Sepandarmaz... .," exclaimed Brian cheerfully.

- "Right . . . Now, I'd better go. You stay here. The less my father knows about you the better."

_ "No, I am coming. I want to know whose daughter I have fallen in love with."

- "Brian, you may get into trouble."

_ "Mitra, I have made my decision. I will meet Izad and talk to it. Why is it going to punish me? I didn't come to this planet on my own accord, did I?"

- "Do you know what will Izad do to me and my family if it finds out?"

Brian took a deep breath, "I will not say you gave me shelter, but anyways, I will come to meet your parents. I have set my mind and I will find a way to take you to Earth."

Mitra surrendered, "Okay, I must change your appearance a bit," she went toward a plant and picked it, "Come on Brian, eat of this so you may look more like us."

Brian chewed the plant and faced the mirror but saw no change in himself, "I have not changed at all."

- "Well, only we can see those changes. Okay, let's go."

And they both went to the door.

They entered an enclosed hall and said hello. Sitting on a chair atop a platform, was a young, tall and handsome man. Without a doubt, Eros was much like his father, and next to him sat a beautiful woman as young and pretty as her daughters. Brian had already met the woman at Hormuzd's party.

At the bottom of the platform, there were six chairs facing each other. Aphrodite was sitting on a chair. There was a vacant chair next to her. Then Eros and Anahita sat, respectively. Based on the sitting order, Brian noticed that the vacant chair belonged to Mitra.

Mitra bowed to her father and sat down. Brian said hello.

_ "Hi, I'm Brian. Nice to see you."

_ "Hi, I am Amortat, and this pretty-faced lady is my wife Mehraveh. Are you an Audit? I have never met you before . . ."

Brian paused and Aphrodite said, "No dad, he is not an Audit. He has come here from Ferdows to study. He was my bedmate in the past, and now I have asked him to come to our home."

"Congratulations," said Amortat with a smile . . .

Brian smiled and fixed his gaze on Anahita's eyes and thought, 'You see? We are all the same in perilous situations. Aphrodite lied easily to avoid exposure.'

Anahita smiled and said, "You are right . . ."

Eros, "Did you say something, Anahita?"

Anahita, "No . . . (facing her father) what a delightful event occurred that we have the pleasure of meeting you this morning, father?"

- "Something went wrong at one of the entry gates."

Mitra asked with fear, "What is wrong?"

- "The guard at the entry gate is missing and a strange object was found outside the gate. We are investigating it."

Aphrodite, "Did you find out anything about it?"

_ "No, we had already come to pay a visit to you at your mother's request."

Anahita, "That made my day."

Mehraveh opened her arms and asked Anahita to get closer. She embraced her.

- "My kind daughter . . ."

Eros quietly whispered in Mitra's ear, ((We must do something soon.))

Mitra, "Let's go to see Ashozushta . . ."

"My beauties, is there any problem?" asked Amortat.

Eros, "No, father. Today we are going to see Ashozushta."

_ "Seriously? That is great . . . Okay, so I go mind my own business."

Anahita, "Aphrodite and I stay with mom."

Eros, "We will take our guest too because he is going to study under Ashozushta."

The kids got up and said goodbye to their parents. As they went through the doorway, Brian looked back at Mehraveh and Amortat and said quietly to Mitra, "They found my ship . . . it smells like trouble . . ."

Eros, "I don't know what you mean but I can't feel happy anymore and I understand you are the cause . . ."

To change the subject, Brian said to Mitra, "It's so nice your parents look younger than you."

_ "We have no wear and tear here. We always stay young and beautiful . . ."

- "Great. So, I will surely take you with me and a young and beautiful lady will be always at my side."

He remembered his dream and went into himself. Eros raised an eyebrow and glanced at Mitra.

Mitra, "Okay, Ashozushta will definitely help you go back . . . ."

He said that to calm Eros down and reassure him that nothing was going to happen, but at the same time, swallowed the anger that had choked his throat. He wondered and rubbed his throat. However, he did not say anything . . .

As the guys left the premises, they noticed the soldiers entering the building. Eros and Mitra felt very anxious and quickly hid behind tall plants.

Brian, "Move, let's go see Ashozushta."

Eros, "No Brian, we must first find out what's going on here."

Brian, "We can go out and make telepathic contact with Anahita like you did yesterday."

Mitra glanced at Eros, "I think it's a good idea."

All three quickly left the building. They wandered for a few hours and then went to a large street, surrounded by green trees, with light shining through the trees and reaching a calm river where two large, beautiful birds with brown wings and the head of a dragon were floating on it. The guys contacted Anahita. Brian strolled around.

As soon as Anahita detected the communication request, she went to the hall of mirrors to be alone.

Eros, "Anahita, tell me what's going on there? What did the soldiers come for?"

Anahita, "I don't know, Eros, but right now dad and the soldiers are going to see Hormuzd."

- "Well, you'd better go too."

- "How can I go, Eros? They will find out."

Eros to Mitra, "She asks how can she get into the royal court since they would find it out anyways. You know, they are the court servants."

Mitra thought for a moment and said, "The invisible shoulder, Aphrodite. . . Tell her to sit on the shoulder and enter the court. No one will notice."

Eros, "Yeah, it's a great idea. Did you hear what Mitra said, Anahita?"

Anahita, "But mom is in Aphrodite's room."

Eros, "I don't know Anahita, find a way and pull her out of the room."

- "But I don't know what to do."

Eros discussed the matter with Brian and Mitra.

Brian, "Well, she can tell a lie and bring her mom out with some excuse. . . Your brains have decayed because you have not practiced such things for a long time."

Mitra and Eros wondered, "What is a lie?"

- "A lie is what Aphrodite told your dad today. I have not come from Ferdows and never been Aphrodite's bedmate."

Eros raised an eyebrow.

- "Well, now that you know the meaning of a lie, Anahita can go and do it easily. For example, she can say the father is waiting for her in the Secrets Room."

Eros, "Mitra, what have you done? Did you take him to the Secrets Room?"

Mitra, "We have no time for it, I will explain later."

Anahita, "Okay. I am going to do that."

Anahita went to Aphrodite's room. Aphrodite and Mehraveh were sitting on the bed talking to each other.

"Mom," said Anahita with fear in her voice, ". . . I think . . . that is, dad . . . said he is waiting for you in the Secrets Room."

Mehraveh, "Waiting for me? But I thought he went to see Hormuzd."

- "Not really. . ."

- "Okay, Aphrodite. I am going to check what your father wants from me and then come back."

Mehraveh left the room and Anahita ran to Aphrodite, "Aphrodite, we need an invisible shoulder. Bring it here right now."

Without asking any questions, Aphrodite began to sing and a yellow creature the size of a buffalo with a cylindrical torso and six short legs and a large eye in the middle of its face approached slowly as if it was floating in the air. Its skin was like that of an elephant and its feet had roots like a tree. It was a little above the surface and made no sound and seemed very calm.

Aphrodite, "Remember, as long as you stay on its shoulders no one will see you or it and you can pass anywhere but as soon as you get off its shoulder, both of you will be visible."

- "Okay, thanks Aphrodite."

Anahita sat on the creature's shoulder and became invisible and made her way to the royal court.

Brian, "Will someone tell me what the invisible shoulder is?"

Mitra, "Brian, I was surprised that you didn't ask a question. The invisible shoulder is a rare creature that, when you sit on its shoulder, both you and it will be invisible."

- "Well, when it becomes invisible, doesn't it make a noise?"

Mitra, "No, the invisible shoulder has no mouth or vocal cords and feeds through its skin."

Brian, "It must be really cool. Well, let's go see Ashozushta."

Eros, "Yeah. Hurry."

And they started out. All the beauties of Paradise were one thing, but as Mitra walked, Brian felt he was in another paradise. He eyed her up and down. The cascade of her hair, the elegance of her loins. Brian had missed the real paradise. He walked a few steps behind Mitra and Eros and watched Mitra. Mitra looked back at him over her shoulder. She smiled and kindled the fire in Brian's heart again. Brian stepped forward and grabbed Mitra's hands.

- "Mitra, I forgot to ask the meaning of your name. Your name is cool. . . It is as the name of ancient goddesses."

- "Ancient goddess? What is that?"

- "Long, long ago, at the time of Adam and Eve, or maybe a bit later, people praised or worshipped a bunch of goddesses whose names were somewhat like yours. Honestly, I don't know much history. After all, you didn't say what does your name mean?"

- "Izad has coined my name and of all the people in Paradise. . . My name means love and affection. . ."

- "Cool, so you look like your name. Well, Eros, what does your name mean?"

Eros, "Izad has named me after the god of love. . ."

Brian, "Izad. . . Izad. . . every moment I get more and more excited to meet it. . ."

Eros, "It is the source of all goodness and wellness. My heart aches to make him angry."

A strange bird was flying in the sky. It looked great and magnificent.

Mitra, "Brian, drop your head down."

_ "Why, what is the matter?"

- Phoenix is on patrol . . . probably the guards have noticed something."

- "What is this Phoenix, by the way?"

Eros, "Your questions have no end, drop your head down and let's go walk under the trees . . ."

Mitra, "Phoenix is a bird with a wide wingspan that lives on a tree called Vispius."

Brian, "There question has doubled. What is that tree?"

Eros replied reluctantly, "A healing tree that contains the seeds of all plants . . ."

Brian, "Well . . ."

Mitra, "Well, Phoenix usually helps out the guards when something important happens."

Eros, "Well, we have arrived and you can ask all of the questions from Ashozushta . . ."

Brian laughed, "Thanks, Eros. You look very logical and reckless contrary to your name."

Eros, "I am very passionate, but my loved ones are my top priority, Brian."

Brian kept quiet, raised his head and saw a beautiful but strange building.

The Castle of Knowledge was not like the buildings Brian had ever seen. The large cone-shaped building, over hundreds of feet high, had a square-shaped building at the top of the cone. One could not see the end of it. The building walls were made of a kind of light ray, and just like the Mitra's Knowledge Room, various typesets were constantly projected on the walls. The walls of the square seemed to be made of glass and were so high that they could not be seen.

Brian, "God, this is fabulous . . ."

Inside the building, however, was different. Many people were walking to and from the building.

_ "It's like a college here, but much bigger . . . I thought Mr. Owl had isolated himself in a dark, damp building and keeps thinking, while now I see he is one of the university professors. My god, how unpredictable everything is here."

Mitra, "Brian, we'd better go inside sooner . . ."

_ "Okay, honey . . ."

All three went into the building together. From the inside, the building did not look conical at all. Space only consisted of doors up to the ceiling. The doors were seventy feet apart and each row was exactly parallel to the other rows. To access the floors, there was a board in front of each door that stopped like an elevator at each floor and the passengers would get out of it and enter the room of their choice.

Brian, "Perhaps, now we have to think about going to Ashozushta's room."

Eros, "No, now you have to find the door to his room and go there on foot."

Brian, "Speaking of what wouldn't it be better to bring Anahita with us instead of Eros? We could laugh a lot as a bonus."

Mitra smiled at Brian, her hand still holding Brian's hand.

Brian, "Okay, where is Ashozushta's room . . ."

Eros, "25th floor, door 3."

They stood in front of door three. They got on the board and went to the 25th floor. When they opened the door, Ashozushta was talking to a young man. Ashozushta's room was large and full of magnificent platforms. A large screen, like a large LED screen, was suspended in the air and sheets of liquid crystal floated in the air. Upon seeing them, the man said good-bye and left.

Ashozushta, "Welcome. Mitra, how are you? Your face seems less radiant."

Mitra, "I am fine. I think the guards know about Brian's presence."

Brian, "The ship that brought me parked at the gate of eternal paradise and I think it that is the cause of the problem."

Ashozushta, "There are no problems here."

Brian, "I need to meet God. There are things I have to ask. There are things that without them I can neither stay here nor go back to Earth. Tell me about the portals . . ."

Ashozushta paused and calmly said, "You have no security clearance and no need to know anything about the portals. I will send you back to Earth without any problem . . ."

- "I have changed my mind; I want to take Mitra."

Eros, "But you have to return Brian . . . alone . . . otherwise, you will get both yourself and Mitra into trouble. You are a child of Adam, doomed to death and Mitra is immortal. Your being together is nothing but pain and suffering. You get old and die and Mitra will watch you decay. She will be sadder every day by missing you and after you, it will be your children's turn to die which she will watch."

Mitra gazed at Eros angrily, "If Izad decides, I can do it . . ."

Eros interrupted her, "To be a mortal? To die?"

Suddenly a teardrop fell from the corner of Mitra's eye, and grief choked her throat.

Eros, "Say something, Ashozushta. Mitra, you are experiencing sadness. That is the result of hanging around with Adam's child."

Brian, "Stop it, Eros. You are disturbing her. We didn't come here for this."

- "No matter why you have come here, go home sooner."

Brian gazed at Eros angrily and turned to Mitra and hugged her, "Don't worry, baby. . ."

Eros, "This is you who are disturbing us, tell Ashozushta how you slept together last night and the night before."

Ashozushta, "No.... !!!! Mitra, did you really do that?"

Brian, "Oh my god . . . Does that mean we are here to talk about this?"

Ashozushta, "Tell me what do you want from Izad?"

- "I want to meet. I want to meet the entity I worshipped as God. You certainly don't expect me to miss the sole opportunity in my life to meet it? I want to ask why it did this to us? I want to know . . . everything. . . I want to know is there any solution for me to be with Mitra?"

Ashozushta, "I will answer your last question. There is no way you can be with someone from Pardis. As Eros put it, you are a mortal and you're being together will beget pain and suffering."

Mitra, "Isn't there a way to make me mortal?"

Ashozushta, "No Mitra, Izad will not accept it. If you turn away from it, you will burn in Hell like Iblis."

Mitra, "I am not like that filthy being. I am not turning away from Izad . . ."

Brian, "Mitra, like Adam and Eve, is a human being. There is a possibility that God will grant her that if she asks for it . . ."

Ashozushta, "Your parents were Izad's dearest ones. They were seduced by the evil Iblis and ignored Izad, now my question is, didn't you want to find a way back to the Earth? I will send you back to Earth."

Brian, "Yeah, I wanted to until last night, but now if I return, return without Mitra, I will never be the same person again."

Ashozushta, "Mitra, Adam's children are free to be fertile or not. You had an affair with a creature outside Pardis. I will make you a potion to abort your fertility."

Ashozushta called his maid. He whispered to her. The maid opened an invisible door and fetched some substances to mix them up.

Brian remembered his dream once again. He quietly said in Mitra's ear, "Mitra, don't worry. To have a child by you is my only wish . . ."

"And about meeting Izad, I don't know whether you will be able to see Izad with this mortal body and those eyes," Ashozushta continued, "But you can definitely hear its voice."

"Okay," said Brian excitedly, "Let's hear its voice. Take me there."

Ashozushta, "But you must promise me you will forget about Mitra."

- "I don't promise to you. Let Izad decide."

Eros, "But Izad will destroy Mitra if it finds out she has slept with you if it finds out she has given you shelter. If you really love Mitra, forget her."

Mitra shouted, "Stop. It's me who decides for myself, neither you nor Brian can tell me what to do."

The maid brought the cup and Mitra gulped it down. Despair overwhelmed Brian's whole being.

Ashozushta, "Go back home now, and come to the temple just before the prayers begin. I will be waiting there for you."

Mitra left the room without saying anything.

Brian, "If I was in Izad's shoes . . ."

Ashozushta, "You are not, Brian . . . You will find out later that all we did was just for your own sake."

Brian nodded in appreciation and went out.

When the door opened, Mitra was standing behind the door.

Eros said, "I stay with Ashozushta. You go keep an eye on the guards."

"Okay," Mitra said calmly with a choked voice.

Both were silent on the way. Brian glanced at Mitra.

- "I disturbed you. I made you upset. In just two days, I came and disrupted your life."

- "Brian, does love always entraps someone so early?"

- "Yeah, two days is already too much. Sometimes, you are entrapped at the first moment you see someone . . . I think love is what destroys a person . . . Mitra?"

- "Yes?"

- "How shall I live with your memories and without you? Why did you drink that potion?"

- "Well, maybe because I didn't know I loved Izad more than you . . . Brian, I can't become a resident of Hell."

- "But you didn't know it is forbidden to fool around with children of Adam . . ."

Mitra lowered her head and kept quiet.

- "Did you know it?"

- "Yeah . . . I knew from the beginning . . ."

Mitra took a deep breath and said, "Maybe, Sepandarmaz . . . you know she is our only hope . . ."

- "So, let's go sooner . . ."

- "I don't think you can teleport your body with the power of the mind. We'd better go home and go through one of the doors, but before that, I must know where Sepandarmaz is."

Mitra closed her eyes and spoke a few words in the Audit dialect. After a while, she opened her eyes and said, "Well, she has gone to the flower garden. We will go to her palace a bit later. . ."

Brian nodded in affirmation and they returned to Mitra's palace and went to Mitra's room. As a person thirsty for water, Brian pulled Mitra to himself and said, "I am afraid each time I am with you, it could be the last time such a thing happens . . ."

And again he poured love into Mitra's whole being. After their lovemaking finished, they lay beside each other.

Mitra, "Let's go, Sepandarmaz is waiting for us . . ."

They got up and headed for the suspended doorway. . . Brian took Mitra's hands and turned her face toward himself and stared at her for a few moments, kissed her cheeks softly and said, "Okay, let's go."

At the doorway, Mitra said, "According to the security clearance authorized by Sepandarmaz . . . Hormuzd's palace hall . . ."

The door opened and the two entered a large hall built on water. Four pillars covered with plants, one suspended doorway from which they had entered, and a golden throne at the end of the hall were all that occupied the space.

A beautiful singing voice could be heard from under the water . . . Brian, who had gotten used to seeing strange things, did not ask a question.

Mitra shouted with her charming voice, "Mooom, . . . I am here . . ."

Sepandarmaz jumped out of the water with her white and shining robe, climbed the stairs that were installed in three rows around the hall, and sat on her throne. Brian stared at her. She looked more beautiful up close.

She had a nice smile on her lips . . .

Mitra bowed, and Brian followed suit.

Sepandarmaz, "Hello to you . . . welcome . . ."

The maids brought a platform for Mitra and Brian, and Sepandarmaz invited them to sit down and then said, "What made my beloved granddaughter come to see me?"

Her voice was soothing and dreamy in Brian's ears . . .

Mitra, "Mom . . . something happened in Pardis that everyone except me was unaware of and more important than that is what has happened to me . . ."

Sepandarmaz waited in silence for Mitra to continue . . .

Mitra continued, "Mother . . . I experienced love . . ." and she told Sepandarmaz all that had happened to her.

As Mitra spoke, sometimes shed tears and sometimes was passionate and all the time her hands were holding Brian's hands, and sometimes Brian completed her sentences.

When they stopped speaking, Sependarmaz, who had been silent all the time, got up from her seat and went toward them and hugged them both for a few moments and said, "My sweethearts... .," she stroked Brian's face and continued, "You are really Adam's son . . . your eyes are similar to him . . . It has been a long time since I last saw him . . ."

Brian, "He is dead . . . destroyed . . . I have never seen him, he died a long time ago."

- "I am sorry, son . . . your father was a wonderful man, he and your mother experienced love too; this beautiful, rare feeling."

Brian said as he repeatedly was kissing Mithra's face, "How can I leave you alone? I am alone in this world. I got stuck among the dastards (he burst to sob like a baby). I am tired, Mithra. Amid incredibility, I am somewhere far away from people, far from home, what is this feeling? I am not so in love that I go and let you get rid of me. I froze up."

- Don't say that, Brian. I don't want to be eternal, or get hurt and sorrow forever for lack of you. I want to live by you, sleep with you every night, wake up with you every morning. I like to go around all over the ground with you. I desire to have a child with you. I will go with you to the ground if God accepts to let me be mortal. I wish I could exile to the earth by eating the banned apple. I want to get to know your mom and meet Albert. I want to know what thing TV is? Or what is the taste of a hamburger? I want to experience all that you said to me last night only with you.

Brian, I was wrong to fall in love with you. I unintentionally wounded in your heart. It is not clear what will happen to me. I dragged you into this trouble (well) with myself.

Mithra, I will stay with you until the end, even if it is eternal suffering. Promise me you will also stay with me.

- I also promise you not to leave you even for a second. I want you to trust me and my feelings. If you don't believe me, I will die in this swamp and the middle of this cruelty. I was afraid, Mithra.

Mithra embraced Brian and uttered, "I will be with you to the end. I will help you."

They spent a few minutes hugging each other, and Brian got a little calmer.

Brian, What are your thoughts on living now? Maybe we can't do that anymore?

- Yeah, it's great. So what should we do?

- Well, imagine, we're on the ground right now, and we're spending a holiday together at home.

- What shape are the houses on earth? Let's make here like there as well.

- Oh, my baby. I say we don't have time. Do you know how long it takes?

- No, it doesn't take time. You paint a picture of the house on this screen. Then, I will call a maid to come here and prepare it immediately.

- How do you call a maid? Maybe she lets the cat out of the bag and reports where we are.

- How many times I have said that our maids are from jinns and they will appear anywhere we will, they pay attention to our commandment and that I do not know what means "let the cat out of the bag"?

- That means she reports where we are.

- No, she's my maid. Even if God asks her, she won't say anything until I don't want to.

- Okay, so say she comes.

Brian took the sheet. The sheet was like a transparent paste. From afar, it looked like a mirror. This time, Brian had so stared at Mithra that he wasn't even surprised by the sheet. Mithra gave Brian a pen that its ink was of light. After you drew, for applying any color you wanted, only tell the pen what color that part of the picture would be.

- Do you know where its good point is?

- Where is?

- When I take you to earth, like movies, you are not surprised to see our technologies, and our lives seem smaller and inconsiderable. Isn't it, Mithra?

- Yes?

- If I die, I have no wish except being with you one more night. It would be so much better. Both of us will feel relaxed.

Tears filled Mithra's eyes. Brian, don't talk like it, we will find a solution for it.

Brian controlled his emotions, So let's see what to paint. First, the kitchen. I think that corner would be the kitchen. Meanwhile, Mithra called for a maid. The maid got present in the hut. Brian designed a kitchen six meters long and four meters wide in the right-hand corner by the entrance. The kitchen was entirely up to date with the cabinets, desk, stove, refrigerator, washing machine, and all of the others.

When Mithra saw the picture, Well, from which material each of them is? Write them down so that Nuno could prepare them like the picture. Brian wrote too, but how could Nuno be able to read my writings?

- Yeah, you're right, so tell her.

Brian started explaining. When Nuno got engaged, Brian defined the bedroom, double bed in a room with six meters long and five meters wide. He designed everything similar to what on the ground, also specified the material of the walls. When he wanted to give Nuno the picture of the bedroom, the kitchen had prepared.

- Oh, my God. It is fantastic, just like what I had in my mind. What a miracle you are, girl? How did you present these with a little bit of power?

Nuno was looking at Brian in silence.

- Look, Mithra. Doesn't she understand what I'm saying?

- Yeah, she does. But she will get happy with my admiration.

- Well, so tell her these are great.

Mithra said, and Nuno happily thanked Mithra's praise. Nuno went to create the bedroom. Brian intended to go to the kitchen, where Mithra prevented him.

- Hurry up, draw the rest. We don't have time.

Brian allocated a place in the bedroom to the toilet and the bathroom. It was time to draft the living room, wooden eight-man dining table with a chandelier above the table, a vase full of red roses, a red carpet had spread underneath the table, with two candlesticks on either side of the table. He placed the TV opposite the kitchen in the right corner and the lower part of the hut. Then, he drew a blue sofa with its wooden front desk.

A chandelier had hung above the sofa. The carpet of this area defined with a navy blue background and turquoise blue flowers.

- Wow, Mithra. It seems she could read my mind. Whatever I imagine, she creates it precisely.

- That's quite right. On this sheet, here is what you think, not what you paint.

- Okay, then why don't I see?

- We could see your thoughts. You cannot see this sheet with mortal eyes, such as we see it.

- Wonderful. All right, we don't have much time, so I am drawing a picture here, a photo of you and me while we are laughing together.

He drew two simple dummies in a painting. He chose velvet cover for the sofa. Nuno prepared the pictures.

- Tell Nuno. I want to receive a signal on the TV. It means to have light, to have a picture, animated ones.

- What kind of images?

- For example, the image of your musician playing in the lowlands, or what else I don't know. Now, we have to give light to these chandeliers. Tell her, hang some light balls of them.

Nuno lit the chandeliers with luminous balls.

- Now, for the kitchen, place the plates in this cabinet, put mugs and cups over there, here is for trays, it is suitable for placing the cylindrical dishes for spices.

As he said, Nuno was preparing everything in a second. Brian asked Nuno to have a cold compartment in the fridge, to generate heat from the gas whenever they pressed its button, as well as to prepare the rest of the equipment so they could use it.

Mithra, But how beautiful and different here is.

- Yeah. On Earth, most houses look like this, simple and convenient. Now, we need only two more things.

- What things?

- Ground specialty clothes and foods.

- Are the ground specialty clothes and food different from here? Ah yes, the clothes you had worn.
- Not precisely that one, but yeah.

Brian remembered his dream. He desired to see Mithra in that shape clothes.

He drafted the clothes. Brian imagined even the white Adidas sneakers he had seen. Nuno created Mithra's clothes, and Brian drew a white T-shirt, green shorts, and white sneakers for himself. The costumes got prepared.

Brian asked Nuno to bring in some dried corn seeds, sunflower seed oil, apples, bananas, and oranges.

- Can she find coffee too?
- Of course.
- All right, then it's all there. Nuno, you can go anymore.

Mithra went toward the clothes she had brought with herself and started wearing costumes. After wearing, from the basket she had with herself, she took out a wreath and laid it on her head.

- Is it beautiful?

Brian, who was ready, seeing Mithra in that dress and the wreath on her head, was about to collapse.

- Yeah, a lot. Very good. You are great. The wreath is also quite beautiful.
- Anahita has made it for me.
- Anahita, what a kind girl. She helped us a lot.
- The only person who I can trust now is just her.

- Come on. I want to hug you. Now, let's not think about anything.

Brian embraced Mithra, "Mithra, I'm just afraid of one thing."

- What?

- It is that you don't know how much I love you.

- Does love have any border and limit?

- Yeah. It is as much as I love you, or I love Ashu zushta[1].

Think about it.

They both laughed together.

Brian, Honestly, I don't want a future that you're not in it. I don't remember life before you.

He put his hand on Mithra's hair.

- Well, pretty lady, you're on the earth right now and my guest. I want to prepare some popcorn.

He grabbed Mithra's hand and took her to the kitchen. He provided the preparation for popping corn.

- Look, learn to make popcorn in this way for me, when we were in the ground. Of course, we have a real television there.

We will rest and watch a movie together.

Mithra lumped in her throat. She lowered her head.

---

[1] Asho zushta is the name of the legendary owl in Iranian myths that eats nails. In Iranian myths, the gods created it to confront the devil. He knows the book, and when he reads the words of the Bible, the demons get scared.

What are you doing, Mithra? Don't worry about it, my love. I will resist all these, and I will talk to God. Yeah, I will find him and talk to him.

- Okay, come on, look at them. They are getting ready.

- Wow, my God. How funny they are.

- Do you know what happens if you remove its lid?

Brian picked up the lid of the pot. Corn grains scattered in the air.

Mithra was standing there, looking at the corn grains.

Brian, What are you doing?

Mithra Coldly, What Should I Do?

- Be afraid and run away from the kitchen.

Mithra acted fear, and both laughed. After popping the corn, they sat on the couch together.

Brian, Well, my love. Tell me what you know very well?

Mithra, lots of deeds?

- As an example?

- For example, like, dancing.

- Okay, dance for me.

- Right now?

- Yeah, let's forget about all our sadness.

Mithra went toward the TV and told the maids what to play. The song played, and Mithra began to dance. Brian was all eyes when he saw her. Mithra's long hair was flying in the air. The fragrance of her hair had filled the room. Mithra was undoubtedly dancing like a goddess. When the dance was over, Mithra stood upright and smiled at Brian.

- How was it?

- Like fresh air, like hope. You are always like these.

- Brian, did you get upset today when I drank that syrup?

- Honestly, yeah.

- I can't say no to God. If he doesn't allow, I can't come with you.

- Why?

- Because if I ignore one who has created me, how would you trust me and be sure I would leave you?

- Brian was in thought.

To change the argument,

- By the way, can you find a safe forest?

- Find what? How could I discover a jungle?

"No. I mean, could you find a safe forest to go in for fun?" Brian laughed loudly.

- Of course. Pardis is so large that anything can found on it.

Brian rubbed his hands, Well, so, call Nuno. She has to prepare something else for us.

- What?

- You summon her to come.

Brian drew the layout, and Nuno made it ready.

Mithra, So what's this?

- It's called a bike. Ask Nuno to create one more of it. I want to teach you cycling.

In the forest,

Brian, Oh, girl. You are so talented! How did you learn while it is the first time you are riding it?

Mithra, It was a slight deed.

- Alright. Well. Can you take your hands off your bike and ride it? This way.

- Mithra followed what Brian was doing.

Mithra, Now, can you take your hand off your bike, close your eyes, and ride the bike?

Brian closed his eyes. Still not a meter away, then he lost his balance and fell.

Mithra laughed out loudly.

Brian, Are you laughing at me?

- Yeah. It was so funny that you fell.

- Well, if you can do it, come on, go.

Mithra closed her eyes and started riding her bike. She rode ahead perfectly.

Brian said to himself, "Look. I just instructed her how to ride; now she has gone beyond me."

He got on his bike and followed Mithra.

On the way back, both were carrying their bikes with their hands, and by walking, returned to the hut.

Mithra, Brian, are you celebrating the marriage on the ground?

Brian laughed,

- Why are you laughing?

- Well, this is also a problem for women, even on another planet. Yeah, baby, we celebrate it.

It is probably the most beautiful celebration of our lives. The ground is not like here that you spend most of the time dancing and having fun. When you wake up in the morning there, you have to work and attempt. Everyone usually works there from morning to night, and family members come together at night.

- Does that mean you and I stay apart?

- No, baby. My job does not need to stay away from you. Maybe one or two hours a day.

- Are not one or two hours too much?

- No, I will take you with myself. Is it good?

- Yes. Well, tell me more about the wedding celebration.

- All right. Your questions are getting more. About marriage, yes, first of all, the bride, the lady who marries the gentleman; we call her, the bride, who has the most prominent role in the celebration. She wears a long white dress with a pretty crown. Mr. Groom usually carries a suit. Would you like it when we reach home, ask Nuno to prepare a bridal gown for you?

- But I'm not the bride.

- So it is possible to try it.

- But here, you can only wear a wedding dress once.

Brian's mind got distracted. What is that, Mithra?

- What?

Mithra looked up at the tree opposite them. A majestic bird with red and golden feathers was sitting on the tree.

- Don't worry. It is a phoenix.

- The phoenix? I have heard something about it in Eastern legends.

- It's true. God sends the phoenix to the ground, but there is only one phoenix in every life period of Adam's children.

- It's interesting.

- Doesn't this bird cause a problem for us?

- No, it cannot speak. We rarely see it. I wonder what it is doing here?

- Let's go home sooner.

At home,

Mithra, Brian.

- What, my darling?

Draw that gown. I want to try it.

- Okay, sure.

Brian drafted the dress, a long white dress with blue embroidery on the border of its skirt, a long white netting with the same blue border, a crown of white gold.

Mithra wore the dress; she looked like an angel walking around with a coquetry. Brian had bewitched.

- Oh, my baby. How beautiful are you? You are the most beautiful girl I have ever met.

- Really? What do girls of the earth look like?

- They are of all kind, ugly, pretty, good, bad, and so on.

- Didn't you like anyone on earth?

- I loved. But I didn't fall in love. I was seventeen years old, and I loved my classmate. Then, I got a friend with her.

- What did she look like? Why didn't you fall in love with her?

- An ordinary girl. We didn't stay with each other much.

- Why?

- Because she went to another country to study.

- Did you get very upset?

- Yeah, I was in my room all a week and looking at her picture.

How did you forget her?

- Over passing the time.

- Does that mean you will forget me over time?

Brian, with a particular naughtiness, Well, anything is possible.

Mithra was staring at Brian with surprise.

Brian burst loudly into a laugh, "Look at her, I'm kidding. How can I forget you?"

Mithra got desperate and sat on the chair.

Brian, My dearest. Maybe someday I will forget myself, but never will you.

And now, the beautiful bride, it is time to refer to the most significant part of the wedding celebration.

- What part?

- Wedding rings.

What are they?

- When a couple holds the wedding rings in their fingers, they promise to spend the rest of their lives together.

- What fun. What do these rings look like now?

Brian designed two rings. He drew a jewel of the diamond on one of them. Inside the rings, he engraved the opposite side's name. Nuno created the rings, and Brian placed the ring in Mithra's finger.

- Okay. You, also settle the ring on my finger, in this way.

- Does that mean we now belong to each other?

- Surely.

And he kissed Mithra. Mithra asked the maids to play.

- Having this TV was quite a good idea; otherwise, we would have to go a long way to reach the music room.

Mithra laughed. Brian, this home belongs to us forever. Doesn't it?

- Yes, of course, my love. How is it that we come here on vacation? We could have a lot of fun. Maybe I would bring my mom.

Our daughter will be familiar with her mother's birthplace.

- Our daughter?

- Yeah, one of my dreams is to have a daughter similar to you, beautiful like Wheatfield.

- Wheatfield? What a pretty resemblance. I had never thought of before.

- Yeah, it's elegant, just like your hair. Mithra, would you like dancing with me like what is usual on the earth?

- With pleasure, but I don't know how I can dance like the inhabitants of the ground.

- Just leave yourself to me. But wait a moment, with these outfits? I think I have to wear more formal clothes. Well, Mr. Groom, I think a black suit is better.

Brian designed the dress and wore it, great and amazing. Mithra enthusiastically glanced at him. Brian took Mithra's hands. He had chosen the tango dance.

As if Mithra had left herself to the wind. She was dancing with him and leaving the world behind. They danced for a few minutes.

- Tell them to stop playing.

- Why?

- Tell them to cut it.

The song stopped, and Brian wrapped his arm around Mithra's waist. He approached her and led her to the bedroom, step by step. He truly drowned Mithra with his kisses.

- Now, I want to share the best night of my life with you.

Mithra's heartbeats were getting increased, and her cheeks had become red. She could feel Brian's breaths on her skin. Brian whispered in Mithra's ear, You are the most beautiful poem I've ever read.

He unzipped Mithra's dress and hugged her and laid her on the bed, then took off his clothes and threw himself over Mithra. Mithra sensed Brian's body with her hand.

Their body movements intertwined as the dance of the waves, and how beautiful their love had combined the two worlds.

- Mithra?

- Yes.

- I love you. I love you. I love you.

I wish these moments were not over.

Brian and Mithra spent several hours in flirtation. The hours went by in a second, and it got evening. Mithra and Brian had lied down in bed in each other's arms.

Brian, I think you should go home so that no one doubts you are with me.

- You're right, but I don't want to go.

- When everyone was having fun, come to me so we could also have fun together.

Brian kissed Mithra's head and hugged her. He wanted to tell her the story of Satan's presence in the hut, but he was afraid, hesitated, and said, "Mithra, in my absence, if the pain of love overwhelmed you, have never taken refuge in Satan."

- I will never do that.

- Well done, my dear.

He kissed her forehead and escorted her out of the hut.

Mithra, Brian, take care of yourself. Have it (an object) with yourself, and blow in it whenever you need my help. It was a necklace with an orb-shaped plaque; the inside of it had designed like the Milky Way.

- So, I will look at it until you come back.

With a smile, she said good-bye while she had no spirit. She went a few steps; when she turned back, Brian was still staring at her. She was not willing to leave him. She turned back and kissed Brian's cheek, then without saying a word, she got her way and went. Brian came back to the hut and then rested on the sofa.

Brian's eyes were about asleep when someone tapped on the door.

- In paradise, no one knocks. Who can it be? Maybe it is Satan again.

He stood back the door, "Mithra, my baby, is that you?"

- No, Brian. Open the door.

It was a sweet, masculine sound. Brian opened the door without hesitation.

A man in a golden-colored dress entered. He was tall and handsome, more than anyone he had ever seen.

Brian, Hi.

The man, Hi, Brian. Welcome to Pardis.

- Thank you.

- Who are you? Maybe. Maybe you are!

- No, Brian. I'm not Satan. Wait a moment; you will understand. How did you see heaven? Do you like it?

- I don't know you; who are you? You know, if you came on behalf of Mithra's father to bring me back to earth, I instantly want to meet God.

- All right, what do you request from God?

- Who are you? Perhaps.

Brian said this, and his heart pounded with excitement.

The man smiled.

Suddenly Brian started describing, Beautiful, beautiful but dull. Well, you know why? We used to work hard and attempt a lot, for whatever we wanted. Having so much affluence and divine blessings indeed make us bored.

The man smiled. What do you want from God?

- My first question is, why were we rejected from heaven because of the sin of our primitive parents?

The second question is, why did he leave us alone, while some of us worship him with passion?

The man, And the last question?

Brian lowered his head.

The man, Come with me.

The man turned on a screen, displaying, a mother and her child had sheltered back of a pillar in a small house. The child was six years old, and he was trembling with fear. The house's door broke, and several men with guns entered. The corpses of a young man and an oldster had fallen in the yard. The soldier kicked the young woman's shoulder and took them out. Then they began mass raping her in front of her son's eyes.

The man, Well, Brian. All your answers were in the episode you saw.

- But many of us do not act in this manner.

- What about you, Brian? Do you behave like this? Do you know the money that you gave the government, has been expended on buying these weapons?

Brian was silent.

- And now, look at this one.

Inside a home, a young man and woman had been on the ground. Brian paid attention more.

- Have they died?

- The man answered with a sad, Yes.

A child who could hardly crawl had been left alone beside his mother's body and cried. Brian wiped his tears.

- Enough, please. Enough! I can't stand it.

- If you were here right now, how was the Pardis? God has only set a test for you, Adam's children, on earth to distinguish the good from the bad. The answer to your question is you, Brian. The son of Adam, you don't even know what disasters are close to happening around you? Governments, powers, and religions are at odds with each other, and only people sacrifice in the meanwhile. Do you think God needs such faiths? Islam, Judaism, and Christianity? All of these are in the interests of powers. The most all-embracing religion in the world is the belief of friendship and love. What do you think the guilt of these women, kids, and men who were defending their homes is? You do not even have mercy on one another, from the same blood, flesh, and skin. How do you expect inhabitants of Pardis would have mercy on your father? Of course, they do so. And now, say, what do you want from God?

- Believe me. I didn't know anything about it.

He put his hand on his knee and sat down.

- I know, Brian. You can't be that much bad man, but you participated in the wicked deeds, all the people on earth are unintentionally partners with their governments and their authorities. With each passing day, you become sadder. Then, you say that God has forgotten you? Intentionally or unintentionally, but it has happened. You have captured by the greed of religions and powers.

- When I go back to earth, I will make up for it. I promise, believe me, I can't be that much bad man.

- I know. But you can't change the earth on your own. And about Mithra, do you know love means sacrifice?

- Yes. I'm willing to give my life to Mithra.

The man laughed, "Sacrifice doesn't always mean dying. Do you know Mithra is an eternal creature and is one of the goddesses of the court of God?"

- Yes, I know, but she can't live without me.

The man laughed again, a loud laugh, "She is an eternal creature. How can she not live without you?"

- You want to hear this. Yeah, it is me that I can't live without her. Does that mean, indeed, there is no way we can be together?

- Being you two together will disturb the balance of several worlds.

So do something for me to stay here.

- We just talked about it; your exam is not over.

- Tell me what I have to do?

- Forget her. Mithra has not experienced grief and sorrow. She has not experienced hardship. Decadence is a nonsense word for her. Also, how can you be satisfied that she is to be left alone after your death?

Brian thought a little.

- You're right. It is absolutely cowardice. I am self-centered. But what would be happened for Mithra? One day this life will be ended for me, and I will bury the loving of her with myself. I will finish, but what about her? She wakes up with this sadness every day and will no literally longer be happy. Have you ever experienced, love?

The man sighed, "Love is so weird. When you fall in love, you think that loneliness will end, and the good days will start. But the more love you get, the lonelier you will be, and the darker your days are."

- When we are together, it's no problem, no worries.

- That's the point. Most people who fall in love don't think about the balance of the world, about destiny and fate. Your world is somewhere on earth. You belong there, and you have to find someone for yourself from there.

Brian smirked, "You have not fallen in love. You don't sense what I'm saying. How do I forget her? How does she forget about me?"

- You will forget, Brian; you will forget. The humankind naturally is a forgetful being.

- Does that mean I might not even remember her one day?

- No. You learn that you can also live happily without her, only.

- Only what?

- Just a reminder, a memory, and a name that wounds your heart every time you remember.

- Well, what can I do with this wounded heart?

- You will put up with it. Until someone comes and heals your wounds.

- No one comes. I know that no one comes.

- Don't be hasty, guy.

- So what about Mithra?

- God will choose a spouse like you for her to relieve her pains.

- The world is full of injustice.

- It is unfair to you. Justice means balance.

- I wish the world would do what we want.

The man shook his head and laughed, Do you know what? One day, you will enter this paradise, sooner or later, when God decides to establish justice for all of Adam's children and bring them from temporal heaven to eternal one. Then you can determine whether to be with Mithra or not.

- Do you know something? This paradise was attractive to me for only two reasons. One is to see God, and the other is that Mithra is here. Will Mithra get married?

- Yes.

- What if she refused it?

- She will accept it. God commands her, and she will admit it.

Brian lowered his head and sighed, "How comfortable. Does that mean everything gets over, and I will come back? As if nothing has happened."

Tears welled up in his eyes.

- You know what? I got finished.

And his tears trickled, he was frequently cleaning the corner of his eyes. He got up.

- Well, then tell her if she accepts I have nothing to say. I only want something; to meet my creator and attend Mithra's wedding party. I want to see it has finished. So maybe I could withstand on the ground.

The man, That would be okay.

Brian silently thought of Mithra, the moments they spent together.

The man, Do you know what surprises me?

Brian raised his head and looked at the man.

- You could demand me many things, such as science, wealth, fame, and convenience. But you ask me to attend the wedding of someone you love her, so hurt yourself more. Adam's children always surprise me. Would you like to come with me to the court of God?

- Of course. Do we see God there?

- Brian, you have met God during your life, even in every single moment on earth. You can't see God with mortal eyes. He was in your every single moment and maybe this moment. Come with me. We will go to the court of God.

Brian was waiting for a miracle in his heart and had dedicated himself to destiny. But he did not want to give up. Brian didn't want to go, but his legs involuntary propelled him. He was confusing and dumb.

They entered the courtyard. It was beautiful and dreamy as if everything were pure gold and shining. Brian was stepping behind the man with glorious and graceful. The water fountains that smelled of flowers refreshed the breath.

The sadness had engulfed Brian's existence and whispered to himself, "No, it is impossible. She will not give me up. But I did it. I did it for the sake of herself." He was staring at the court; a memory passed through his mind.

It was night, the door of the mansion knocked on. It was raining. A man wearing a suit and carrying a black umbrella was standing in the back of the door. Brian was nine years old. He looked up from the top of the fence. One of the maids opened the door.

The man, Hi, I wanted to talk to the owner of the house.

Brian's mother and grandma went down the stairs. The man was sitting in the living room; he got up by seeing them.

- Hello Mrs. Werner. I'm sorry I came here late time.

Elizabeth asked with anxiety, What has happened?

- Unfortunately, we got informed that Mr. Werner has died in a car crash.

Tears trickled from Grandma's face. Her mother sat motionless on the sofa and gazed forward. Brian was coming down the stairs when he heard the news. He stood on the fifth stair.

- My dad.

Grandma noticed Brian's coming. As she was wiping her tears, she opened her arms, Brian, my baby, come here.

When he recalled that moment, he closed his eyes and sighed sadly. The man who had read Brian's mind pulled his face, but he continued on his way. Brian would remember the bitter memories of his life as he went ahead, the moment when his grandmother died while he was a teenager, the moment that his father's bankruptcy announced he was a twenty-one-year-old. He had been trying for months to keep the company and his family afloat.

He whispered with himself, "I went through all of these troubles. Then I can also handle this."

The hall with all the greatness and glory was dark in Brian's eyes. As if something was collapsing inside him.

- What am I doing here? I am a stranger here.

He had dedicated himself to destiny. Come what may. He only wanted to get rid of this uncertainty. It was as if he was in deep trouble. He smirked.

- The man without looking behind him, What are you laughing at, Brian?

- At that, I got stuck in paradise.

And then he burst into bitter laughter.

They entered a hall with no column. The sky was blue, and there was not even a piece of cloud in it.

There was a throne, king-shaped one, above the hall. Mithra and Anahita were standing in a state of respect. The Amertat and a few other men were facing them and near the throne. The court was luxurious. Brian heard the sound of several steps behind himself; he looked behind himself. Mehraveh and his two other daughters were coming towards the court from behind them. A bird descended from the sky; it was the phoenix. The eternal paradise beings had come to the court to see Adam's son, from angels to humans, goblins, and other creatures. Brian stared at Mithra. In this short time, she had gotten lean and gaunt in his view. His eyes were exploring as if he was looking for someone. The throne of

God was empty. The excitement of seeing him made Brian forget about love. He was thinking to himself, "Maybe he is on the throne, and I can't see him."

Surprisingly, he noticed that the man was with him, climbed up the stairs, and sat on the throne.

"What! You! Are you God?" Said Brian while he had his eyes on stalks. Yeah, I guessed correctly from the start. But you, you are humankind. Is God who we worship him a human?

God smiled, "Everybody discovers me differently; you can't perceive my real self. Here no one sees me as you see. Everyone sees me as much as he/she can understand me, not as I am."

And then he commanded in a clear voice, "Guards, close the gates. This meeting will hold between the servants and us." It was the first time that God was investigating an issue related to a creature behind the closed doors. The guards closed the gates.

Brian, unaware of the surrounding space, suddenly came up with a sound. It was Anahita who had bowed her head and called God.

- God, God, let me speak.

- Say, Anahita.

- God, why don't you do a miracle for them? They can't stay without being with each other.

God, What do you imply by the miracle? You mean that either Mithra becomes mortal or she accompanies Brian in the earth and stays eternal. The marriage among the worlds is forbidden.

Anahita, But God, Brian can be immortal.

- Then, what about justice? Brian's test is not over on the ground.

Mithra had stared at the floor all the time.

Brian, Mithra, why don't you say anything?

Mithra, Just like you. You were silent when God asked you. What did you say?

Mithra said in a sad voice while tears coursed down her cheeks, "My opinion is in line with the will and the rule of God, quite the same as Brian."

Brian intended to explain to Mithra that he had done all this for the sake of herself, but when he saw the tears and pride in Mithra's eyes, he preferred to diminish a part of this love by his silence.

Anahita, What are you saying, Mithra?

Amertat, Anahita, don't interfere. Apologize to God and go out.

God, It is not needed. Amertat, it is Anahita's favor. But Anahita, I will explain to you the reason for all my decisions after exiting all. But about you, Mithra, this evening you will be married to a boy from the floor of Light House.

Mithra's legs got feeble.

The guardsman who was there asked with surprise, "But, God, how can Mithra get there? While no man or woman with thousands of years of worship cannot easily get there."

God looked at the man, and the man lowered his head as a sign of respect.

Mithra's tears became more intense. She thought of Brian. With her eyes, she asked him to say something, but Brian averted his gaze from her.

God, Final comment. Until Brian finishes his test and returns to eternal paradise, Mithra marries a boy named "Ash" from the Light House clan. After Brian's returning, if they both wish to join again, Mithra can divorce from Ash and marry Brian. Brian, after your return, if you let Adam's children know about Pardis, you would be rejected from heaven forever.

Brian, When will I come back?

- According to the promise you got, tonight after Mithra's wedding ceremony, with the same device you have come to Pardis, you will go back.

- But what about fuel and the other issues? The ship needs repair.

God smiled, Everything has reviewed and resolved, and you don't need to be worried.

God said this and left; everyone bowed to him. Brian was standing and watching his exit. He whispered to himself, "Is that the only time I saw you? How can I live without you and Mithra from now on?"

Everyone left, but Anahita and Mithra were standing in their place. Mithra stared at Brian with great anger.

Anahita, Why didn't you say anything? Both of you? Brian, why did you keep silent when God came to the hut?

Both were silent. Brian kept his head lowered, and Mithra was still looking at him. After a few moments without exchanging words, Brian left the hall and headed for the hut. He was panic, just like all the tough moments had passed, but this time harder. Maybe in the past, he thought that suffering was no worse than it was at that moment. But one's pain and suffer diminish after a while. Brian got out of the court; all the people were still behind the door; Aras was also among them. Brian didn't come down the stairs. He stood there and had a look at the crowd and shouted, "The people of Pardis! The immortal creatures! I don't know how many of you know yourself superior to my father, Adam, but I want to tell you that no one of you is better and cleaner than him. Guys, you are cowardly creatures who sacrifice everything for your comfort. Being with you is a pitiful matter. I am glad that I am going to come back to earth and not seeing you. I am glad my father went to earth. Whatever we have, we have gained it. Our love for God, even if it is a little, is more precious than your sense for him. You are a pack of hanger-on persons who would perish if God forbade his blessings from you. You are poor people who have never experienced love, and I am sure if you were in my dad's situation, you would have behaved worse than him."

He said this, angrily stepped down the stairs, stood beside Aras, gave him a cold look, and uttered, "What you did to save yourself and your family sounds admirable, but to me, you are a miserable creature who has only the name of love out of it." He said this and moved promptly to the hut. Everyone was staring at him in silence and opened the way for him. On the way out, he would scream, break down the branches of the trees, and immediately a new growth would emerge. Heaven was like a cage where he had trapped in it for a lifetime. The joy of jumping and not knowing to fly had driven him into madness by the time of freedom. Without love, he had no wings to fly. The thought of Mithra's eyes, her smile, her lips drooped him downward. He sat on the floor and cried.

- Even God is also opposite to me and cannot help me. What kind of love is this? Gosh, help me to forget it. Oh, my God. Why me? Why?

A man driving a chariot approached him. Brian didn't raise his head; also, he didn't pay attention to him.

The man, The son of Adam! God told you to wear these clothes for the wedding ceremony. In the evening, two fairies will come to pick you up and take you to the wedding party.

He nodded his head in approval and started crying again. This time he was not able even to sit. He didn't put his hands on the floor either. He stayed there in that position for a long time.

Suddenly, the lovely voice of God heard, I know you are confused. Come with me to a place where nobody could go there after Adam and Eve.

Brian was scared. He didn't expect God to be there.

God urged Brian to stand behind him, and at one blink of eyes, both appeared elsewhere.

Brian, What happened?

God laughed, You are in accompany with me, Brian. And anything is possible in this status.

Brian had a look around, But it's a sea.

- Yeah. Eve loved this place very much.

- I also love the sea. It makes me calm down. Look, did you create the sea on the ground because of Eve?

- Let's say that because the earth was more in tune with their moods, I sent them there.

- Why didn't you forgive them? Why didn't you ignore their sin when you love them so much? Why didn't you ever go to see them?

God sat on a rock and stared at the sea, "It is very complicated, Brian. I am the God of the world, and I must be fair. What would have happened if I had forgiven them?"

Brian, You're right. But why did you love them more than anyone else? Before them, humans were in paradise. Why do you have to recreate a being?

- It seems Adam and Eve are like other humans. The humans who created before Adam also any other creature in the universe came to life by my breathing, which I blew at their dry body. But when I created Adam, I removed a part of myself and put it in his body. After I saw no human being was able to perceive him, I created a peer for him and left another part of myself in Eve's essence.

Brian sat beside God and also stared at the sea, "I think I can understand this matter. It must be something like a maternal sense. A mother shares a piece of her existence with the child that comes from her."

- No, Brian. It is much more profound. It is like slicing yourself and your soul. A part of my soul was spoiled when Adam and Eve became ephemeral.

- Well, when they left their mortal body, did you get your essence back?

God, It was too late. My essence was passed on to their children and also from them to the next generation. My soul got several thousand pieces.

- So we are all part of you, and you will not feel comfortable until we all come back to you.

- Right. It has been a long time, and I have not created any creatures after Adam and Eve.

"I'm sorry we have made you so disappointed," Brian put his hand on the one of God.

God put a hand on Brian's head, "The greatest sadness of the world is that you want to behave in a fair method. You have to sacrifice lots of things when justice is in your hands. Do you like that we stroll calmly?"

- It is a good idea.

They both stood and began strolling along the sea.

Brian, Did you know something?

- What?

- You are more lovely than I thought, also simpler and kinder. Believe me! I didn't deem you would have such sadness. You know that you are God.

- Well, you are the first person to hear this from me.

- Didn't you tell the others? Didn't they know you are so sad?

- Even if they know it, they will give me no sign. You know I'm their God.

He said this and smiled.

Brian, You didn't tell them because you were afraid of hurting your pride.

God wiped away the tear that was dripping from the corner of his eye. Suddenly the sky got cloudy, and the sea became turbulent.

Brian stood up and hugged him, and everything calmed down in the blink of an eye. He couldn't believe he was embracing his God.

- My pride hurt when I got betrayed when pieces of my essence do not have mercy on each other. Some of you have blackened the spirit so much that when you turn it back to me, I can no longer accept it.

Brian, I don't know about the others, but I love you. You know, when I am with you I forget all my problems. In my opinion, the sadness of love is not that profound too. I know you won't accept it but if you like I can stay with you.

God had a cackle, "You created a lot of trouble in that short time. If you stayed longer, I would probably have to deport all Pardis' creatures."

Brian laughed, You're right.

- By the way, tonight you have to wear particular clothes. Are you sure you want to attend?

- Yeah, if I don't go and see this, this love will crush me.

- You won't have a comfortable night.

- Will you stay with me?

- I'm always with you (referring to Brian's heart), here.

Mithra was in her father's house and in a room where stairs went up from there into the sky. She had stared at a moving image of the galaxy mounted on a wall of gold. She dressed in red-colored clothes that had made of light. It seemed the dress had decorated with diamonds.

Her forehead was painted by several gold-colored motifs, and having a beautiful, green crown over her head. The tear that was ringing in her big eyes was similar to a sea in which sadness was surging. A voice caught her attention. It was Brian; he was standing in the corner of the room, wearing a white dress for the celebration.

- How beautiful you have become!

Mithra proudly raised her eyebrows, staring at the wall so that her tears would not flow.

- What are you doing here? Who has led you?

- The only friend I have here, Anahita.

- What do you want?

- Come with me, Mithra, we will go to earth.

- I can't.

- I will make a great living there for you.

- I can't.

- Come on, Mithra. We will be happy together.

- Yes, but only for a short while. If God doesn't allow me to be a mortal being, you will die after a while and go back to Pardis, and I will stay on the ground forever.

- I said these things so that you know that whatever I did was for your own sake.

Meantime, a sound like a trumpet tone heard. The beautiful fairies came from the steps of heaven down to the floor. In their hands was something like a basket with strange objects. They came to Mithra as they were cheering, and they ringed around her. They brought a carpet and allowed Mithra to sit on it; Mithra couldn't control her tears. Four strange blue-colored birds grabbed the corners of the carpeting and flew. Brian followed the fairies. The fairies were ringing around the rug, and the carpet was flying over their heads. Mithra turned back and had a look at Brian; Brian lowered his head. They passed through the garden and reached Mithra's family. The birds grounded the rug, and Mithra got off it. Her parents also her sisters and brothers were waiting in a line for Mithra to pay tribute to them, and then hand in hand with her father went into the bridal chamber. But Mithra indifferently passed her family away. As if she had not seen them. She went straight to Brian, paid tribute to him. Brian kissed Mithra's forehead.

Mithra, Now that you like so much to see my marriage, lead me to the bridal chamber.

- No, Mithra. Don't ask me this work I can't stand it.

Mithra stood behind Brian and held his hand slowly.

- You have to go straight to reach the bridal chamber.

- Brian set out. Mithra was overwhelmed in seeing Brian, Mithra's family followed him, and the fairies were cheering behind them. The sound of certain music had filled the space. It was halfway through, which Brian felt he was not able to continue. He had a glance at Amertat, released Mithra's hand, and headed in the opposite direction. Amertat grabbed Mithra's arm, but Mithra was looking backward. Mehraveh took her other hand and took her to the bridal chamber. Brian didn't go to the marriage room. He was waiting outside. He didn't know what to expect; maybe it was a moment for saying goodbye to Mithra.

The bridal chamber was in the middle of the hall, and everyone was standing around it. Ash was sitting on a chair among the crowd. He was handsome and appealing. The birds mounted Mithra on the carpet and turned her around Ash. Mithra closed her eyes and wished that Brian was sitting in the chair. She was thinking about the hut and one day of life which they spent there. The birds laid the carpet in front of Ash. Mithra raised her head and looked at Ash. Then she lowered her head.

Brian was sitting in the garden. God came quietly and sat down beside him.

Brian, I don't know why I miss all my sadness when you come to me.

- I am always with you. Brian, be patient, it will end.

- Are you going to stay with me till the celebration is over?

"Brian, when you go back down to the ground, the memories of here may bother you. Try to be strong," God smiled.

Brian smirked, "How to be strong? You knew I didn't believe in you very much, in heaven or anything else base on religion. But now, look, I am in the middle of this truth like a prisoner."

- You are the son of Adam, good or bad. You love to search. When Adam's children enter the eternal paradise forever, we will also experience a new sense in here. And about your belief, indeed, I am aware of all parts of my soul. Moreover, I must say I'm glad you didn't get involved in something ridiculous, called religion.

- I thought faiths were very significant to you.

- I didn't deem you were such stupid. That's what they call religion. Which one of the beliefs brought you the truth? The faiths that built have caused war and animosity between you and made me even more heartbroken.

- Sepandarmaz said that before him, some people had come here through the passageways, are they the prophets?

- Yeah.

Did they succeed in meeting you?

- No, they only saw Gabriel.

- Why did you build that passageways on earth?

- Well, when the angels went down to guide Adam, they had to come back, so I made these ways.

Brian stared at the hall and said, "I wish it would end sooner. You knew something I supposed you had a scary figure! But you were utterly kind. I didn't think I could talk to you so easily. Take care of Mithra, if you see she doesn't like that guy, don't urge her to live with him.

He wiped his tears and continued, But what should I do? What can I do? What? Help me not go crazy there.

- Brian, don't forget that you have some half-finished works on earth. You owe to the people you unwittingly oppressed them, also to the people who have drowned in foolishness called religion, race, and power.

- I know, when I come back, the first thing I will do is going to Syria and helping its people. I would love to find that child and would adopt him. When I come back, help me with any signs to discover him. OK?

- The kid you saw represented a lot of other kids. Maybe you can help them somehow.

- What do you think of an equipped orphanage?

- It's a good idea. Do something to get some peace. War is the worst thing that happens between Adam's children. You are the only creatures that fight your fellow man. Think about which kinds of animals or creatures have behaved like you so far.

Brian thought.

- I have created you being the perceptive creatures to promote good and to learn the difference of being good or bad, not to be hungry for power, and to oppress.

Brian laughed. I say, assume that if we were still here, we would put it in soil and blood.

God laughed bitterly.

- Are you disappointed with us?

- If I was desperate, there was no trace of Adam's children now. Till a child of you is born, I still have hope for you.

- Do you think the wedding party is over now?

- Yeah, Ash is a great guy. Maybe he can relieve Mithra a bit.
- To be honest?
- Yeah, say.
- While I haven't seen him, I hate him. I tell, how many days last that I have been in Pardis up to now? It is for about five days; is it right? But it seems like I have spent a lot of time here and with these guys, but do you know where its sad part is?
- Where is it?
- I am still hungry for seeing Mithra. What can I do with this hungry? Where can I have a complaint from you?
- It was a decision you made, other than that is?
- That's right. The grand point of this story was that I realized you are always with me.

God put a hand on Brian's shoulder and filled his soul with peace.

- You should go and get ready. Brian, it's time to leave.
- Don't I see Mithra anymore?
- Yes, you will see her. They will bring Anahita and Mithra near the fourth door to have goodbye.
- Anahita, what a kind girl!
- Sometimes her courage reminds me of Eve.
- Can I lonely go to the gate? Saying goodbye to you is the hardest thing in the world. I'm afraid to see you and can't come back.

- Do you know the path?

- No.

A chariot came towards them.

- Get on this vehicle; it will take you there. Your clothes are also there. Anahita and Mithra will arrive as long as you do your works.

Brian got on the chariot.

- One more thing.

- What is it, Brian?

- I say, come to my sleep sometimes; we are just two of us. This matter won't make a problem.

God laughed; OK, Brian. Come on, go. When you get out of here, you can call the earth and announce that you are alive.

Brian raised his hand as a sign of goodbye.

"Can I especially tell these matters to my mom," Brian said as the chariot departed from God.

- Of course, you can tell it to your mother and even your partner.

Brian, now farther away, shouted, "I want you to know that I love you with all my being."

He turned his face and headed towards the gate. On the way, when he reached to places where he had spent time with Mithra, he paid more attention to them to have a picture of their being together in his memories. He reached the tree, that was hiding behind it and had seen Mithra for the first time.

- "Exactly at this point in life, my destiny changed forever; Goodbye heaven."

He reached the gate, and the guards opened the gate. He saw the spacecraft in front of the gateway. He went into the shuttle and wore astronauts' clothing. When he exited off the shuttle, Mithra and Anahita were standing there.

Anahita asked with a loud voice, Brian, let's say goodbye. I have to go.

- So what about Mithra?

- She stays a little longer.

Brian hugged Anahita and said goodbye.

- Anahita, having a sister with you made sense to me. Thank you for all the hard work you put into it.

Anahita shed tears. Take perfect care of yourself. I have heard the ground is a dangerous place.

- Don't worry. Not that very bad as you have heard. I will miss you.

Anahita got into a chariot and left. Mithra was silent, and her head was down. She bent over and paid tribute to Brian.

- Brian, your love bud will remain in my heart forever; I am waiting for you to come back. Know that I will never give up on any man.

- No, Mithra. I don't want that. I only want you to live and be happy. Promise me.

Brian wanted to hug Mithra. But he was ashamed of her marriage, and he pulled himself back.

- Mithra, remember something forever. From now until the time that I breathe, I will spend every second with the thought of you. When I come back here, I like to be in love with me like now.

"Go, Brian. I cannot stand anymore," Mithra burst into a sob.

- I won't say goodbye to you.

Brian put his hand under Mithra's chin and raised her face.

- Let me have another look at these big eyes. Because after that I won't see all that much beauty.

- I beg you, go.

Brian kissed her forehead and walked towards the ship.

Mithra shouted, Brian, take care of yourself. Brian, I love you so much.

Brian, however, did not look back that if he did, he might never have left. The guards grabbed Mithra's feeble hands and took her inside Pardis. The gate was still open. When Brian reached up the stairs, he turned back and had a look at Mithra. Mithra raised her left hand and showed him the ring that Brian had put in her finger. Brian smiled bitterly and looked around. He sighed and boarded the spacecraft.

- Mithra, without you, only I remained of us.

The wind blew and made the blossoms to fly. The guards closed the door, and Mithra fell behind the door.

- God, keep Brian's heart pounding and make his journey safe.

The ship was turned on and was ready to launch after a few minutes. God was hiding outside the gate behind a sturdy tree. He sighed after launching the ship, and I suppose, if God had a beating heart, it would have stopped, when Brian left Pardis as if the spirit has gone of his body. How lonely was our Lord!

Brian, I wish everything were asleep.

After leaving the atmosphere of Pardis, Brian began contacting Tom and the organization.

- Tom, Tom, do you hear my voice?

He tried several times, and after a few minutes, he received an answer.

- Hello, Brian Werner.

- To who am I talking?

- It is Susan. Brian, are you indeed yourself?

- Hello, Susan. Yeah, it is me. I'm moving toward Earth's orbit.

- What are you saying, Brian? We haven't heard from you for about six months now; how have you been alive? Where did you get your spacecraft fuel?

- Wait, please. When I meet you, I will explain everything. I want to get everything ready for my landing.

- Okay, Brian. Don't worry, no problem.

Susan quickly reached out to her colleagues and shared the news she had received. A lot of noise arose in the hall. Tom moved quickly to the communications facility, "Brian, dear Brian, do you hear me?"

"Yes, Tom. I can hear your voice," Brian sighed coldly.

- Thank God. How are you, guy? I can't believe; where have you been during this time?

- If you like to hear, I'm well, no; I'm not, Tom; I'm not well.

- I'm preparing for your landing. There are many things you have to tell me.

- If I can say it and if you can believe it.

- What thing?

- Nothing, Tom. Nothing. I ask you for a request.

- What do you want, my son?

- Tell my mom that I desire her would be the first person I will see.

- Okay, sure.

Tom contacted Elizabeth, and the mansion had taken over the atmosphere of enthusiasm. Elizabeth moved quickly to the organization. In a short time, many journalists and photographers gathered there. All the politicians associated with Brian and all the girls who somehow tried to get him were present with big bouquets.

The spacecraft landed four days later, and Brian got off it. He looked around; Tom and some of the staff were waiting for him at the landing zone. How weird he was on earth that he didn't even feel the nostalgia. Tom embraced Brian. "What's up, Brian? Where were you? Where have you been so long?"

As they were moving to the lounge hall, Brian replied, "Tom, don't ask me anything; I don't want to talk at all."

- Okay, I know you are tired, but for now, you should explain it all after you rest. When they arrived at the lounge, a lot of noise arose. He was looking for someone, among the people until he saw his mother, she was standing in the crowd and crying.

He turned around to his mother and embraced her, no matter what.

Elizabeth, Oh, my son, my lovely son, my life. Where were you? Over this time? My life is over.

- You cannot imagine what happened to me; you cannot imagine. Mom, I am so tired, take me out of here.

- Okay, my son.

Amidst the commotion of the crowd, Brian barely moved to his car without speaking a word. The driver opened the car door, and then Brian and his mother got in his car.

Days passed, and Brian was thinking of his lost love in his loneliness. It was as if the ground was a small and dark place for him. Her mother asked for the reason of his grief, and Brian told her the whole story. Elizabeth was looking at Tom while she was stunned.

- Mom, how can I live by experiencing this love and whatever I saw?

- My dear son, you really can't live with such great pain. You went to heaven and came back again. You fell in love, and most of all, you saw your faith with your eyes. I know it's hard, but you are Brian Werner; you are a strong man who went through many difficulties. You will pass through this matter.

- Mom, I will go crazy.

Elizabeth hugged Brian, "No, my son. Be strong, baby."

- My days have been dark and cold since I came back. Mommy, I am going to make up for the wicked deed I have done. I am going to dedicate a part of our fortune to the war-torn Syrians and Afghans so that maybe I can compensate for some of the cruelty they have suffered.

- Great, my baby. It is an excellent idea.

After that, Brian arranged for help, and that calmed him down a bit, and it was a slight relief to his endless pains.

Seven months and two weeks had passed since Brian's return, and in the meantime, Brian had imprisoned himself in his room, and all he could do was, standing by the window and looking out.

Repeatedly, Tom and many of his close friends came to visit him. But his tired soul couldn't bear to see anyone. It was as if he had just brought his body to the ground, and his soul left with Mithra and God. In the evening of that spring day, the air strangely smelled of heaven. He opened the window. His appearance was untidy or disheveled.

- Gosh! You said I forget; you said it fades. So why not? Huh? Why not? Answer me.

He started shouting, "God, I am talking with you; do you hear my voice? I know you hear. It has not faded; it will not fade." He said these words and wept. He began to break the stuff in his room. There was so much noise that the maids entered the room quickly. He shouted angrily, "Get out, get out. No one comes into my room without my permission" then, he sat on his knees.

- God! my soul is tested every day, and my mind stays fixed every day. How can I forget? Her hands, her eyes, the smell of her body, and her voice. How can I forget? I mean you, you. Oh, my dear, I left you alone and came back. I won't forget. You are not forgettable; you will not fade. Where can I escape to calm down a bit?"

Suddenly a thought like a thunderbolt struck Brian's mind. He remembered the stuff he had brought from Pardis. He hadn't looked for them since he came back. He had forgotten or perhaps feared not to find a trace of them. He recalled the necklace which Mithra had given him in front of the hut.

He remembered Mithra's words.

- Whenever you want to talk with me, ask it of this necklace. Then I will come to you wherever I am. He quickly went to his wardrobe and brought out the backpack with his belongings.

He took out the camera; its battery was over. He connected it to a power outlet. But there was no hope that there would be a movie. He turned the camera on and sat on the floor by the power outlet. Surprisingly, he noticed that all the videos he had taken on Pardis were still inside the camera.

- How could it be possible? I thought, after I come out of there, God will not let me bring a sign with myself.

He played the movie that had recorded at the party night, and when it reached the picture of Mithra, Brian began to cry.

- Oh, Mithra, my love. How did I not see this movie in these past months?

He kissed Mithra's picture. He put the camera aside, held the necklace between his two hands, and blew at it. He didn't know what was going to happen. But he wanted to do it, and he did.

Seven years later, Brian was writing on his father's Russian desk in his workroom. The painted image of Mithra was right in front of him. In his laptop, he played a video of his lecture at a university held among a large number of students. Brian forwarded the video a little, turned up the laptop volume, and listened carefully to the speech,

I'm Brian Werner. I'm here today to talk with you. Have you ever thought about what the most significant thing in this world is?

The power? The races? The countries? The borders? The religions? Which one?

Why are we so apart? Why has this unnecessary prejudice about religion, faith, race, or country made us so apart?

Where are we going, and when are we coming to ourselves?

I am here to tell you I have been all over the world to find out that the most valuable thing in this world is love and affection. What is the significance of being a Christian or a Muslim? Jewish or Zoroastrian? The important thing is to be good. It doesn't matter what skin color we have. The issue is our hearts (souls) would be white.

The criterion of supremacy is not the color of the skin, the religion, and the country. Tell me which one of you did you choose these features when you were born?

It's a long time that we have forgotten brotherhood and equality. We all have the same parents, Adam and Eve.

How do you let that your brother gets oppressed around the world?

The war was the only result of these differences. Let's win once. Our enemy is war. We must win that, a dream of having a united world together.

Let's make this dream a reality. Believe me. We don't have to fight for world peace. (The laughter of the audience rose.)

Yeah. That is the utmost ridiculous work we have ever done, the war for peace. Peacefulness can only create calmness. What does it matter what religion you have? Religions have come to lead us to God. But believe me, God is not also pleased that you would have enmity with your fellow man because of the religious differences. Please open your eyes and look at this world away from any prejudice. The most significant thing in this world is purity and integrity. It means to be well persons and do good deeds for your fellow men. Believe me. That would be enough for going to heaven.

The problem is that we have forgotten the owner of the house in the middle of this house. Yeah, we have lost God. I admit that peace is more troublesome than war because you have to change your beliefs to be the right person. But for a moment, think about this how trivial these differences are if we get attacked by another planetoid. We will all work together to defend our planet.

The united earth, what a beautiful expression! Let's do well and scratch each other's back. Let us love each other no matter what the differences we have.

We hold a thing in trust; it is the soul that God has donated to us as a white tablet. He has given us his spirit. Let's be careful about it, so when we return it to him, we play a beautiful role in it. The audiences cheered.

The door of Brian's room opened, and a five-year-old baby girl with golden hair and a blue and pink shirt entered the room. Brian turned off his laptop. She was the girl of his dreams.

- Dad, come on, hurry up. So when are we going?

Brian smiled with eager, "Right now, my lovely princess. Let's see where your mom is? Is she ready?"

- Yes, I'm ready.

Brian turned his head, a woman with big eyes and black hair. She had a beautiful and innocent face. She was simple-dressed and stylish. The short black dress and long hair on her shoulder had increased her beauty.

- Catherine, my baby. How beautiful you get!

- Thank you, my dear. Your mom is waiting; She says that by ordering the driver, we first reach her to the mall before setting out to the airport.

- Okay, darling. So, hurry up. Otherwise, we will lose the flight.

In the car,

Elizabeth, Brian, how is your book writing proceeding?

- Almost done, mom. I'm thinking about its title.

Catherine, I found a good title for it, "I went to heaven and returned."

Elizabeth, Yeah. Meaningful, my baby.

Brian was staring at the outside of the plane. The drizzling rain hit the window. He closed his eyes and thought about the moment he blew at the necklace. That scene appeared just like a live image in front of his eyes.

At that moment, he blew at the necklace then Mithra's voice was heard from across the room.

- Brian, you are the most beautiful blessing that God has ever granted to me. Before you, life had no color and meaning. I don't know how beautiful the singing of birds was before you? Or how subtle was the flower? I only know that I didn't live before you. When I get out of here, there is no longer a relationship between us. I'm glad I was able to live with you for one day. I haven't had a better day than that in my life, and I live with that memory and feel happy until you come back to me. Brian, I hold your love like a light in my heart, and this light keeps my life bright until you come back to me and start our eternal life together. God has decided to send me somewhere, full of joy. There is no sadness there, and I try to be happy with your memories. I also ask you, if you indeed love me, strive for your life and happiness; but never forget me. Let's be happy and lively until we could meet each other again. Brian, here are some things I want you to do for our love.

First, you can't finish the mortal world loneliness, so get married, make love, and have a child. When you feel comfortable, so do I. Dear Brian, happiness is the only thing I ask God for you.

Secondly, there is a book you need to find it that gives you eternal peace. Go to the east and look for that book.

Brian, I spend every moment of my life with the memory of you. Your fragrance changes my mood, and my heart fills with love by remembering your look. I always go to the house we built together and take care of it until the day we could go back to our home. Our worlds may be far apart, but our hearts will never be far away. So don't let this separation accede you. Get up and go on with your life.

The voice of Catherine brought Brian back to himself. "I hope the east has many sights. I am sure we have an exciting journey ahead."

- Of course, my dear.

- Yeah, mom. I searched a lot in cyberspace. Be sure we have an exciting journey ahead.

Brian and Catherine both laughed.

Brian stared at outside. That was the only thing left of Mithra's requests; finding a book and discovering a new world.

www.ingramcontent.com/pod-product-compliance
Lightning Source LLC
Chambersburg PA
CBHW072134170626
46813CB00004BA/1556